I0573792

Once Upon a Wish

Pam Andrews Hanson

CRIMSON
ROMANCE
Avon, Massachusetts

This edition published by
Crimson Romance
an imprint of F+W Media, Inc.
10151 Carver Road, Suite 200
Blue Ash, Ohio 45242

www.crimsonromance.com

Copyright © 2012 by Andrews and Pamela Hanson

ISBN 10: 1-4405-5234-7
ISBN 13: 978-1-4405-5234-2
eISBN 10: 1-4405-5233-9
eISBN 13: 978-1-4405-5233-5

This is a work of fiction.

Names, characters, corporations, institutions, organizations, events, or locales in this novel are either the product of the author's imagination or, if real, used fictitiously. The resemblance of any character to actual persons (living or dead) is entirely coincidental.

Dedication

FOR RALPH, AS ALWAYS.

CHAPTER 1

"Mandy, are you sure you don't want to wear your glasses? You'll miss seeing your own wedding?" Amy Crane held her cousin's thick lenses, trying to persuade the soon-to-be bride to put them on.

"You're my dearest friend and my maid of honor, but you just don't understand." Mandy patted the vivid red curls piled high on her head. She'd spent the morning at Wonderful Waves, the only beauty salon in Heart City, Iowa. "I want Judson to see me as the most beautiful woman he's ever known. Fifty years from now when I'm old and gray, he can look back on our wedding and remember how gorgeous I was."

"Judson Carter has been your boyfriend since the eleventh grade. He must love you with glasses, or he wouldn't be marrying you," Amy assured her, although it was no use trying to change Mandy's mind when it was made up.

"I do wish you'd gotten used to contact lenses," Mandy's mother, Linda Ferguson, said. "Your father did offer to take you to an eye specialist in Des Moines to see if you'd have better luck."

"Mom, they hurt my eyes. Anyway, I've been wearing glasses so long, I feel naked without them."

"All the more reason to wear them when you walk down the aisle," Amy pointed out, giggling with her cousin.

"Anything I can do to help?" Amy's mother asked, poking her head into the small room in the church used by bridal parties.

"Aunt Alice, you can find Hannah before she rips or soils her pretty little flower girl's dress," Mandy said. "Have you seen Judson's little brother? I can't possibly walk down the aisle unless he holds my train."

You could if you'd wear your glasses, Amy thought, but she

didn't say it. This was Mandy's day, and whatever made her happy was okay.

The bride finally stopped peering nearsightedly into the only mirror in the room, so Amy moved in front of it to catch a quick glance. The two bridesmaids were wandering around somewhere in sunny yellow gowns with adorable little jackets, but Mandy had insisted Amy wear a shade of green that reminded her of the pet frog she'd had in third grade. It did absolutely nothing for Amy's honey blond hair and deep blue eyes, but if it made her cousin happy, she could tolerate it for one evening.

The door flew open and Hannah bounced into the room, her flower girl's halo of silk flowers hanging precariously on her blond curls.

"People are coming! Daddy and that tall boy are showing people where to sit." This wasn't seven-year-old Hannah's first wedding, but it was her first opportunity to star as the flower girl.

Amy smiled at her sister Natalie's daughter and wished weddings were still exciting for her. Most of her friends were married, and she'd lost track of how many times she'd been a bridesmaid. No way did she regret getting her pharmacy degree while most of her high school friends were getting married and pregnant, but weddings were an emotional roller coaster as she watched everyone she knew taking the plunge.

"Let me fix your halo," she offered, trying to secure it without pulling her niece's long curls.

"I need my basket of flowers," Hannah said with the self-importance of a child suddenly elevated to stardom.

"Your mom will give it to you when it's time to walk down the aisle," Amy assured her.

"This is just like a fairy tale," Hannah said, waxing eloquent while Mandy reclaimed the mirror to check out what had to be a fuzzy image of her face. "When I grow up, I'm going to marry Prince Charming."

"I wouldn't be a bit surprised if you did," Amy said, smiling at her adored niece.

The organ began playing, and the wedding party hurried to the narthex. When the wedding began, Hannah took her own sweet time scattering flower petals down the aisle, the groom's attendants looked as if they'd enjoyed the bachelor party too much, and Mandy's father stuttered with nervousness when he had to say his piece about giving his daughter away.

When everyone moved to Veterans' Hall for the reception, Amy breathed a sigh of relief. Her cousin had been duly wed without tripping on her train, and Amy had gotten through the ceremony without any waterworks, a first since she was prone to crying when friends tied the knot.

She lost it when the bride and groom cut the cake, and Mandy nearsightedly smeared frosting on Judson's neatly trimmed blond mustache and beard. Her cousin was a married woman now, and one more of Amy's childhood friends would be starting a family of her own.

Her eyes swimming with tears, Amy rushed through the back exit and found herself on a paved area behind the building, a basketball court where the vets worked with youth. A security light made eerie shadows but was hardly needed. The June moon was huge, and stars flickered in the sky like distant fireworks.

Amy dug into the front of her bra for her emergency tissues. Of course, it was silly to cry at each and every wedding she attended, but by all accounts, her Great Aunt Beatrice had been the same way. People in town had sometimes left her off guest lists because of her tendency to bawl louder than the minister could talk.

After some careful blotting, Amy's tears dried up, hopefully without smearing her mascara until she looked like a raccoon.

"Don't cry, Aunt Amy. Some day you'll marry Prince Charming. Then you won't have to cry."

"Hannah, I didn't hear you come outside!" Amy was startled and more than a little embarrassed because her niece had seen her weepy episode. "I have something in my eye, is all."

"You shouldn't fib," Hannah said self-righteously. "Mommy says lies hurt people."

Yes, that sounded like something her sister would say, Amy thought, although she had to admit her older sibling had been a perfect child—when adults were watching.

"Oh, look!" her niece cried out in excitement. "I saw a shooting star!"

Amy peered at the sky, but if there had been a falling star, she'd missed it.

"You can make a wish on the first star of the evening, but wishing on a falling star is even better," Hannah said. "I'm going to make a wish for you."

"Oh, no, you should make one for yourself." While Hannah was looking upward, Amy dropped her damp tissue. She felt guilty about littering, but she didn't want her niece to notice it. Maybe she could pick it up when Hannah went inside.

"I wish Aunt Amy will find a Prince Charming to marry, and I want to be the flower girl," Hannah said in an earnest voice.

"You're a sweetheart," Amy said, reaching down to hug her niece. "But wishes don't always come true."

"They do in fairy tales," the little girl insisted. "Especially if you wish on a shooting star. It happens all the time."

It happens in stories, Amy thought. She cried at weddings, but it didn't mean she was unhappy. She loved her job as a pharmacist at Warner's Drug Store, and when the owner retired, she fully expected to take over the business. Because Heart City was a small town with no major roads leading to it, Main Street was still a viable shopping area. The pharmacy did well, and Amy took great pride in the role she played in the town folks' health.

"Hannah, what are you doing out there?" her mother called from the doorway. "I've been looking everywhere for you."

"She's been with me," Amy said, knowing it was better to pacify her sister than argue. She loved her, but Natalie wasn't exactly flexible.

"I need both of you," Natalie said. "Mandy is ready to throw her bouquet."

Groaning inwardly, Amy dutifully went to the hall where the bridesmaids in yellow were ferreting out all the single women under the age of ninety. Even though she'd caught the bouquet at three other weddings, Amy knew it was futile to beg off. Instead she stood at one end of the group, hoping Mandy would throw it straight at the girl in the middle instead of at her.

"Is everybody ready?" the bride called out, blinking to focus because she was still refusing to wear her glasses. She'd have to watch the wedding video the groom's Uncle Jake was shooting to know what happened on her big day.

Several teenage girls squealed and jockeyed for position, but Hannah managed to get in front of them. If she caught the bouquet, would she give it back to Mandy? At some weddings, it was the job of the maid of honor to secure and return it, but Mandy hadn't asked her.

"Here it comes," the bride called out, turning her back for an impartial toss.

Only then did Amy remember her cousin pitched in a softball league. Yellow roses and white carnations became a flying missile as she threw with gusto—right into Amy's face.

"Oh, I'm so sorry," Mandy said, rushing over as cries of alarm spread through the losers. "You're bleeding!"

Amy let the flowers fall to the floor and reached up to assess the damage. Who knew bridal bouquets came with enough wire to pen a herd of cattle? Her fingers came away with a smear of blood, and she could feel it trickling down the side of her face.

"Get Doctor Prince," someone behind her cried out.

A practical wedding guest grabbed a handful of the napkins printed with the bride and groom's names in silver and handed them to Amy so the blood wouldn't stain her dress.

"I'm fine, really," she insisted, more embarrassed than hurt.

"You're bleeding like a stuck pig," Joel Hayes, her sister's husband said.

"Head wounds bleed a lot," one of the bridesmaids said, as she flitted around Amy.

"Do we have a wedding casualty?" a deep masculine voice asked from behind her.

Hannah rushed over and tugged on Amy's free hand. "It's Dr. Prince. He gave me a shot. It hardly hurt—well, not very much."

Amy turned and met a pair of blue eyes so vivid it was like plunging into the lake on a sunny day. As if they weren't enough to take her breath away, the man peering at her forehead had a picture-perfect mass of curly black hair and the body of an athlete. His exotic cheekbones, nicely sculpted nose, and strong chin would make him stand out anywhere, so it was particularly unnerving to see him in Heart City.

She knew there was a new physician in town, but, surprisingly, no one had mentioned he looked like a Greek god. Of course, he'd been there such a short time, he hadn't even phoned in a prescription during her shift at the pharmacy.

"This is a first," the doctor said, gently lifting the wad of napkins from her forehead. "A wounded bridesmaid."

"Maid of honor," Mandy said, hovering close and looking distressed. "Dr. Dan Prince, this is my cousin, Amy Crane. I feel so bad about this. You told me to wear my glasses."

"It's okay, Mandy. I'm sure I'll live, and it will give you one more wedding memory," Amy said, wishing people would stop staring at her.

"Keep pressing the napkins and come with me," the new doctor ordered. "I didn't bring my bag, but there's a first aid cupboard in the kitchen."

"Good thing I invited the new doc to the wedding when I went to see him for—a little problem." Judson flashed a slightly guilty look at Mandy, but of course she wasn't seeing anything very clearly.

Dutifully following the doctor to the area where the vets prepared their famous pancake breakfasts, Amy was feeling increasingly silly. Of course, she'd wanted to meet the new physician. It was a very big deal for the town to have him practicing in the offices old Doctor Graham had occupied before retiring.

Unfortunately, Dr. Prince would only be there two years. A special program had paid his medical school fees in exchange for two years of practicing in Heart City. In the kitchen, his short tenure seemed especially unfortunate for the town when he charmed the hovering bridesmaids, calmed Mandy down, teased Hannah, and worked on her forehead, all at the same time. The man had talent, and it wasn't all medical.

"You won't need stitches. It's only superficial," he said. "Next time duck."

Some bedside manner, Amy thought, feeling like a sideshow exhibit as more people, including her mother, crowded into the kitchen.

Patching her up only took a couple of minutes, but making an escape from the crowd was trickier. They weren't there to see her. Everyone in town was curious to watch the new doctor in action. No doubt his appointment schedule would fill up fast now that so many women had seen his tall, dark, and handsome good looks.

"Is it going to scar?" her mother asked.

"Highly unlikely," the doctor said. "Is that music I hear?"

The small three-piece band, seldom-employed musician friends of Judson's, had started to play.

"How about we have the first dance?" Dr. Prince asked Amy. "Show people you're not seriously wounded."

Apparently he didn't know the bride and groom were supposed to have the dance floor to themselves for the first one. Or maybe it wasn't a custom in Santa Barbara, California, where he'd grown up. Amy was surprised she remembered that fact, but his life history had been front-page news in the town's weekly newspaper.

"I don't think . . . "

She really didn't want to dance, not with all eyes focused on the doctor, but he took away the option of refusing. Taking her hand, he led her out to the open area in front of the band. Her discomfort grew when even the bride and groom stood watching. Poor Mandy! Even though she didn't seem to realize it, she'd just had her big day hijacked by a California cutie who just happened to be the town's temporary physician.

"I don't want to steal the spotlight from the bride and groom," Amy whispered, all too aware of his hand on her waist.

"I suspect you already have," he purred close to her ear. "I never could understand why brides pick their prettiest friends for the wedding party."

If that was his idea of a compliment, why did it sound like teasing? Amy tried to concentrate on following his lead. She knew what was to come. The whole town would be buzzing for weeks about the way the doc had swept her off her feet, and she'd spend half her working time at the store explaining it meant absolutely nothing.

So much for enjoying her cousin's wedding!

CHAPTER 2

Dan questioned what he was doing as he took the pretty little accident victim in his arms on the dance floor. He'd sworn to himself not to get involved with any women in the little hick town where he was fulfilling his obligation. He was totally focused on getting back to California and joining a practice that would allow him to enjoy the sun, surf, and relaxed lifestyle on the coast.

"Your name is Amy, right?" he asked. She seemed to float across the floor in his arms as the amateur band hammered out a sentimental number.

He liked to dance, but short women were usually hard to lead. His ideal partner was close to six foot, only a few inches shorter than he was.

"Amy Crane. I'm a pharmacist at Warner's Drug Store. Maybe I should sit down. I feel a little dizzy."

"Don't worry, I won't let you topple over," he said, wondering even as he said it why he wanted to finish the number with her. "Did you pick that dress yourself?"

It was none of his business, of course, but he couldn't imagine a worse color to go with her lively hazel eyes and halo of dark blond hair. Or a worse color—period.

"Goodness, no! My cousin—the bride—insisted on it."

He didn't rub salt in the wound by telling her he'd dissected something that color in freshman zoology. In fact, he was trying to be on his best professional behavior even though he felt like a fish out of water in the small Iowa town.

"So, Pharmacist Amy Crane, how long have you been working at the drug store here?"

"Not quite three years."

He'd pegged her as barely over twenty, but when he calculated the years it took to get a pharmacy degree, he was surprised to learn she was only a couple of years younger than he was.

"What made you decide to work in Heart City?" He was genuinely curious. She could probably make twice as much in a hospital or pharmacy in a bigger city.

"It's my home. My mother's a widow, so I wanted to live fairly close to her."

"Yeah, I can understand that. I was raised by a single mom."

He was exceedingly proud of his mother. She'd worked her way from being a temp at the museum to executive secretary to the director. His father had been killed in a multiple-car pileup on the freeway when Dan was only four. His memory of him was fuzzy at best, mostly based on photographs his mother still kept on display.

The music ended on a sour note, but he had to give the three-piece combo credit for trying. He'd been wondering how the people in Heart City made a living, but obviously it wasn't as musicians. So far, he thought the town existed mostly to provide shopping and services for farmers. Already in June, the fields around the town were shades of vibrant green as corn and soybean crops pushed through the rich, dark soil. The rural scenery was pleasant to drive through, but he had no clue what people did for entertainment.

"How long have you been here?" Amy asked as she walked beside him to the chairs lining the utilitarian beige walls.

"Just a couple of weeks." He marked off every day on the Norman Rockwell calendar his part-time nurse assistant had given him as a welcoming gift. He didn't know whether this would make the time seem to go faster or slower, but he liked to keep track of time.

"Did you find a nice place to stay?" his dancing partner asked.

"Nice enough, yes." What could he say about a bedroom the size of a supply closet and a kitchen that was part of the living room? It was the back rear apartment in a large Victorian house that had been chopped up into five units a long time ago. At least the rent was cheap, and he was all about saving money until he could get back to Santa Barbara.

When Amy-in-the-awful-dress was seated on one of the folding chairs, it was his cue to thank her for the dance and leave the reception. Although he appreciated the invitation, this wasn't his kind of party. Everyone seemed to know everyone else, and he was more a curiosity than a guest who belonged there.

Instead he sat down beside her, although he wasn't sure why.

"Still dizzy?" he asked because it was the only excuse he had to hang out with her.

"No, I'll be fine."

"You're the first maid of honor I've seen injured in the line of duty," he said with a smile.

"It wasn't Mandy's fault. She's practically blind without her glasses."

"You're a good sport about it." He reached over and pressed the tape on her bandage more securely to her skin, a totally unnecessary gesture. Was it his fault he felt protective?

"Can I get you something to drink?" He remembered seeing a punch bowl with green foamy stuff in it.

"I'd really like a glass of water," she admitted diffidently, as though it was too much to request of a stranger.

"Maybe some cake too?" he suggested as he stood to get a drink for her.

"Maybe later, thanks. I'm a little put off by inch-thick frosting," she said with what could be a sheepish smile.

"Did you have dinner before the wedding?" He surprised himself by asking.

"No, but I'm not hungry. All I really want is to get out of this dress."

He arched his eyebrows, knowing what a California girl would mean by that.

"No, I didn't mean . . . " Her cheeks flushed, and she shifted her bottom on the hard chair seat.

"Yeah, the color doesn't do anything for you," he said to lessen her embarrassment. "I'm going to grab a burger at that diner on the edge of town. Care to join me?"

"Thanks, but I still have to help Mandy get dressed to leave on their honeymoon. She'd be disappointed if I didn't stay."

"Where they going?" He couldn't care less, but against his better judgment, he wanted to prolong their conversation.

"Herbert Hoover's birthplace in West Bend, Iowa. Judson has always wanted to go there."

Dan had to stifle a laugh. Of all the places to honeymoon, Hoover's historical site would be on the bottom of most people's list. Of course, small-town folk were a different breed, one he was only beginning to know.

"I'll get that water," he said.

What he didn't anticipate was how long it took him to get back to the kitchen. One elderly woman tried to consult with him about arthritis in her hip. Two giggling girls asked if he'd be giving physicals to their school soccer team. The groom sidled up and told him his little problem was better.

By the time he got back with a plastic cup of water, Amy Crane wasn't where he'd left her. He surveyed the crowd, feeling a little foolish fetching a drink for a woman who wasn't there.

Maybe it was for the best. She was cute, especially for a pharmacist. They tended to wear wire frame glasses and carry pen protectors in their shirt pockets. At least that was his impression in Iowa City, where he'd gotten his medical degree. The last thing he needed was a crush—make that an attraction—since he was looking at turning thirty in a couple of years.

"Oh, you brought the water," she said coming up behind him. "I thought maybe you'd left."

Did she think he'd offer and then duck out? Was that the way a man treated a lady in Heart City, Iowa? A lady! Would women in this town like being called that, or was it as politically incorrect as it was in metropolitan places? He had a lot to learn about small-town life in the Midwest. Unfortunately.

"Thanks," she said, draining the glass in one huge gulp. "You have no idea how thirsty I was."

He did now, but at least she wasn't at all pretentious, sipping as if more than an ounce would wash her away.

"Will your wife be joining you here?" she asked, taking him aback. Why did she think he was married?

"Not any time soon, since I don't have one."

She'd managed to hit a sensitive subject. His longtime college girlfriend had broken up with him rather than join him in Iowa. It was for the best—their relationship had been going downhill fast—but it was still novel for a woman to break up with him, and he didn't like the feeling of being dumped.

"Well, there's not much for a single person to do here. The Methodist Church has a singles group. We're fortunate to have a movie theater that shows second runs. There's a roller skating rink but it's mostly a hangout for high school kids." She recited the town's attractions in the flat tone he associated with the heartland of the country.

"Guess it's good I'm here to work, not play. I take it you're one of the singles." He was fishing, which was ridiculous given his determination not to begin anything he'd regret when it was time to leave.

"I am single, but I don't go to the singles group. I've heard they're mostly retreads—divorced people looking to try again or single parents."

"I guess that would count me out too. Sure you won't join me for a late night snack? I missed lunch, and those little cream cheese sandwiches won't fill me up."

"They're watercress sandwiches. Mandy read in a book that the English are big on them. But no, thanks. I can't leave this early. It's in the maid of honor's rule book."

"Too bad, but thanks for the dance. You won't be getting a bill for my first aid."

"Big of you. Thanks," she said in a flat voice.

He'd meant it as a joke, but it came out wrong. She'd probably think he was a money-hungry carpetbagger, and she wouldn't be totally wrong. After scrimping his way through medical school and his internship, he looked forward to having a little extra cash—and keeping up the payments on the seven-year-old van necessary to his practice. According to the terms of his contract, he had to visit patients in the county hospital approximately seventeen miles away. There were also elderly people who might require a house call, a tradition still alive in rural Iowa.

"Well, it was nice meeting you, Amy," he said.

"The same here. People are excited to have a doctor again, even temporarily. I think you'll like us when you get to know us."

Did he come across as a misanthropic? Her comment stung a bit. He'd honed his bedside manner until he could be as warm and fuzzy as any doctor.

"Well, see you around," he said, deciding it was past time to cut off this conversation.

"Just so you know for future reference, Warner's a full-service drug store," she said. "There's a soda fountain and a post office substation along with an extensive inventory of pharmaceuticals. If we don't have something you prescribe, either Mr. Warner or I will drive to another town to get it at no extra cost to the patient."

"That's good to know." Her spiel sounded like a commercial, but it was good information. "I'll see you around."

Or maybe, he thought, I'll try to avoid you. So far she was hands down the most attractive woman he'd seen in Heart City. This might be a lonesome gig, but he didn't want his life complicated by romantic attachments.

CHAPTER 3

"I don't have to ask if you had a good time at the wedding," Josie MacDonald said when Amy unlocked the front door of the pharmacy Monday morning.

"Why wouldn't I have fun? My dress was as flattering as a potato sack, and I was wounded by the bouquet." She went about the process of opening for the day, turning on the lights while she pretended not to know her friend was talking about the infamous dance with the doctor.

Josie had been a good pal in high school, and they'd renewed their friendship after Amy got her pharmacy degree and started working at Bert Warner's drug store. Like many who graduated in Amy's class, the popular blond cheerleader had never left Heart City. Instead, Josie married the high school quarterback and settled for a job clerking in the store.

"Don't by coy," Josie teased. "Everyone in town knows you were the only one who danced with that hot new doctor."

"He was only checking to see if I was all right after I was scratched by the wire in Mandy's bouquet." Amy self-consciously touched the small bandage on her forehead, more a token reminder than a necessity.

"A dancing doctor? If that's how he examines patients, he's going to be the busiest physician west of the Mississippi River," Josie said with a little smirk.

Josie was grinning when she went behind the soda fountain to start the first of several pots of coffee. Warner's was a popular place for work breaks as well as an evening hangout for teenagers. Bert professed to hate the soda fountain business, but he believed it brought a lot of people into the store.

"I was a little dizzy—oh, never mind," Amy said, going to the pharmacy department at the rear of the building.

Fuming a bit at Josie's ribbing, she clipped her nametag on the pocket of her starched white jacket, not that all their customers didn't know her already. Bert said it made her look more professional.

No doubt, Josie was only the first of many who would comment on her dance with Dr. Dan Prince. She wasn't looking forward to explaining to customers who came into the store, not that anyone would believe how impersonal his attentions had been. Her niece Hannah wasn't the only one in town who thought she should find a fairy-tale prince.

Bert was more excited than anyone else by the arrival of the new doctor. When people had to go out of town for medical appointments, they were more likely to have their prescriptions filled at one of the big superstores. Of course, Warner's Pharmacy had a number of loyal customers who wouldn't trust anyone but the owner for their medicine, but Amy was gradually building trust among them. In fact, the first customer of the day was Mrs. Grady, an octogenarian and outspoken, but sometimes amusing, longtime resident.

"Well, what do you think of him?" she asked as she stomped up to the counter thumping her cane. Usually she banged her empty pill bottle on the counter to indicate she needed a refill, but today she only stared at Amy through big round owlish glasses.

"Are you here for a refill?" Amy asked, pretending she didn't know the elderly lady was fishing for gossip.

"Fiddlesticks! I've got enough of those pink pills to last 'til I'm ninety. Hope that new doc has enough sense to put me back on the little white ones. They're a lot easier to swallow."

"Can I help you with something else?" Mrs. Grady wasn't the easiest customer, but most of the time she amused Amy.

"Tell me about the new doctor! What do you think of him?"

"I'm sure he's very competent. He graduated from the University of Iowa Medical School." It wasn't part of Amy's job to evaluate medical caregivers, but she knew the elderly woman wouldn't give up until she said something.

"Oh, I know all that—everybody does. How's his dancing?"

"Please . . ."

"Give it to me straight. Is he as smooth as everyone thinks?"

"He's very . . ." Amy looked up and was stunned to see the subject of Mrs. Grady's curiosity standing right behind her.

"Very what?" Dan asked in a teasing voice.

"This is Mrs. Grady," she said to avoid answering. "She has arthritis and high blood pressure. She may decide to consult with you."

"I'm Dan Prince," he said, graciously extending his hand to the elderly lady. "My dancing is only fair, but I'm great on a surfboard."

Amy had an instant vision of the tall, muscular doctor riding a big wave under the California sun. It was a disturbing thought, and she quickly erased it from her mind.

"Pleased to meet you," Mrs. Grady said, putting her withered hand into his. "Never heard of that surfing thing in Iowa, but the HCCC has a big carnival every July. They're always looking for someone who doesn't mind water to sit on the dunking machine."

"I'm afraid it would be a waste of the doctor's time," Amy said, still embarrassed by his sudden appearance.

"Harvey La Font got an ear infection from being dunked a couple of years ago, but folks don't much like him," Mrs. Grady said, ignoring Amy and keeping a firm hold on the doctor's hand. "There was a big line waiting to have a go at him. He's an outsider, came from Dubuque to run the fast food place on the edge of town. A word to the wise: I've heard they mix horse meat in their burgers."

"I'll keep that in mind," Dan said, laying his other hand on top of the elderly woman's. It was a kind gesture, but it also reminded Mrs. Grady to let go.

"Well, I'll be on my way," the old woman said with a suspiciously flirtatious smile.

"How can I help you?" Amy asked when the doctor stood alone on the other side of the prescription counter.

"You can tell me what the HCCC is." He grinned mischievously.

"Heart City Community Center. It's a hangout for retired people. You'll probably be asked to do blood pressure screenings or diabetes testing there."

"That I'll be happy to do. I may pass on the dunking machine."

"Good call," Amy said, smiling in spite of her reservations about the new doctor. "Is there something I can do for you?"

That came out wrong, she immediately realized, when she saw the gleam in his eyes.

"For now, you can fill this scrip. I was cleaning out brush behind the clinic and picked up some poison oak." He extended his arm to show her some nasty red blisters. "Apparently I'm super sensitive to it."

"It doesn't look too bad. Are you sure you don't want to treat it with over-the-counter remedies like antihistamines and calamine lotion?"

From the look on his face, she could immediately tell he didn't like being second-guessed on medications.

"Sorry, of course, you're the doctor," she said, embarrassed by her goof. "When there's no physician in town, people tend to come here for medical advice. Older people, especially, won't travel out of town for an appointment if I can sell them a patent medicine to relieve their symptoms. Of course, I urge them to see a doctor most of the time."

He was one of those people who could send messages with his eyes. Amy squirmed under the intense glare of his dark eyes and hurried to fill his prescription.

Ordinarily she would ask whether he had insurance for the prescription, but she was so jittery under his gaze she forgot. Fortunately, he had cash lying on the counter by the time she bagged his medication.

"I hope this helps," she said, meaning to be polite.

"Do you doubt it will?" he asked.

Was he trying to intimidate her? She snapped out of her timid mode. If there was one thing she'd learned from friends who were nurses, it was that doctors could be bullies with their subordinates. Well, this newbie M.D. wasn't going to get under her skin. She'd suggested a cheaper, safer way to treat his rash, and she didn't need to apologize for it.

When she moved away without answering, he got the message.

"Sorry to snap at you," he said. "This rash itches like crazy, and I have my first appointment in less than an hour. My patients won't have much confidence in a doctor who's scratching."

"Good point," Amy conceded.

"I didn't ask how your head is," he said in a more mellow tone.

"It's fine, thank you."

"Like I said before, I have to admit you're the first maid of honor I've known who got hurt by a bouquet." For someone who was tormented by itching, he didn't seem in a hurry to leave.

She'd forgotten how tall he was. Bert should keep a wooden box for her to stand on behind the counter so she could deal with long, lanky customers who looked like movie stars on an eye-to-eye basis.

"If there's anything I've learned working here, it's that people can get hurt almost anywhere," she said, resorting to chitchat to relieve her feeling of awkwardness. "My cousin's new husband had a run-in with a fishing hook that nearly scuttled the honeymoon."

She'd wanted to impress him with her worldly knowledge, but she instantly realized she shouldn't have gossiped about something Mandy had told her in strict confidence.

"I know a little about that," Dan said.

"Sorry, I shouldn't have said that. Sometimes the town's mania for gossip rubs off on me."

"I take it you won't feel a need to broadcast my run-in with weeds." He picked up his prescription and turned to leave.

"Of course not!" she snapped, more irritated at herself than him. He did intimidate her—just a little—but not because he was drop-dead gorgeous or smart enough to be a physician. There was a big city aura surrounding him that made her feel like a country bumpkin. Why had he landed in their small community?

Oh yeah, it had to do with the town's desperation for a doctor and the extremely high cost of getting through medical school. But that didn't explain why a California hunk had landed in small-town Iowa. Her intuition told her he was going to spend a miserable two years fulfilling his obligation, but his attitude made her mad. Heart City was a nice place. Good people lived there. No one had the right to look down on them.

"Have a nice day," he said as he walked away.

That was her way of saying good-bye to customers. He left her with nothing to say as she watched him walk away—although his slender waist and firm backside made that a visual pleasure completely unconnected with who he was.

"What did he want?" Josie hurried up to her as soon as she had a break from serving coffee and donuts to the guys on break from the lumberyard.

"You know I can't discuss customers with you," Amy said, more weary than annoyed.

"Well, I saw him walk out with a prescription bag, but there can't be much wrong with such a fine specimen of manhood," Josie said with a grin.

"Please!" Amy looked toward the front of the store, hoping someone would bring her a prescription to interrupt this conversation.

"I wanted to come back and meet him," Josie went on, oblivious to Amy's reluctance to talk. "But wouldn't you know, Ken and Billy kept going on and on about how we always run out of bear claws before they get here. It's not as if I place the order for donuts."

"You have another customer at the front," Amy pointed out.

"Oh, it's only Mrs. Cornwall. She'll spend twenty minutes

picking out a lipstick then realize she forgot her purse and can't buy it this trip."

"Well, I don't want to talk about Dr. Prince," Amy said. Sometimes a person had to be up front with Josie.

"I don't know why not. There hasn't been such a stir in town since the pep club's float tipped over in the homecoming parade when we were juniors. Remember how it messed up a pickup truck? My, that farmer was mad!"

"With good reason," Amy said, glad Josie had changed the subject. "Whose idea was it to build a replica of the Eiffel tower on the roof of a Volkswagen?"

"Well, certainly not mine," Josie protested. "I thought we should do a scene with the cutest football players in uniforms. That would include my hubby, of course."

"Mrs. Cornwall is waiting to pay for something," Amy said. "Remember Bert's motto!"

"Yeah, I know. GTM. Get the money. Can't pay the bills if we don't sell anything."

Josie hurried off to wait on the customer, and Amy couldn't help but smile. If an accident in the homecoming parade was still on her friend's mind after more than ten years, it was no wonder an outsider would find life dull in Heart City.

It was no concern of hers, though. Dr. Dan Prince was gorgeous, but he probably couldn't wait to get back to sunny California and all the bikini-clad beauties on the beaches. As far as she was concerned, that couldn't happen too soon for her peace of mind. She didn't even want to think about him as a surfer in a skintight suit with water cascading over his broad, tanned chest and shoulders.

Hopefully she wouldn't require more first aid from the hunky physician. She'd have to be especially careful to avoid illness, injury, and invitations that put her in range of Dr. Prince Charming.

CHAPTER 4

As Dan hurried through the rear entrance of the small building housing his practice, he didn't know what was annoying him more: his itchy arms or the encounter with Amy Crane. It was a truism in his profession that doctors made lousy patients, but he hadn't expected a pharmacist to suggest alternate medications.

He ripped open the small white sack from the drug store in the privacy of his office, dabbing the powerful ointment on his poison oak. Sitting at his desk with his eyes closed, hoping for quick relief, he tried to think of something besides the petite blonde. She wasn't his type, even if he were looking for a relationship, which he definitely wasn't.

Had he made a mistake accepting Heart City's financial help in exchange for two years of his life? Now that he had to fulfill his obligation, it would be easy to dwell on his regrets. Certainly, he was eager to move back to California, and he had hopes of getting a residency there after he served his time as a general practitioner in Iowa.

"Be honest," he chided himself, knowing he would've been swamped with debt without the financial aid. After the years of hard work to become a doctor, he should be able to do two years in Heart City with no sweat. The one thing he absolutely had to do was remain aggressively single with no entanglements with local women.

As he slipped into one of his neon lab coats, he still felt itchy and, face it, threatened. He should be thinking about his first day on duty instead of dwelling on Amy. Sure, she'd annoyed him, but he wasn't thin-skinned as a rule. The way she looked in her little white jacket was much more disturbing. It covered her assets and made her look professional, but she was still beguiling in a cute sort of way that had never appealed to him before. So why couldn't he get her out of his head?

"Dr. Prince?" His nurse assistant rapped sharply on the office door. "Are you ready to start seeing patients?"

Georgia Stewart was a semi-retired R.N. who'd agreed to work with him during his two-year stint. She was a plump, chatty older woman with fluffy gray curls and seemed to be über-efficient. After working with the former doctor, she knew office routine better than he did. If Dan could tune out her constant stream of town gossip, he should be able to rely on her professionalism.

"Almost ready," he called out, wanting a few more minutes for the itching to subside.

His assistant popped her head into the room, looking a little startled when she saw him.

"Dr. Graham always wore a white coat," she said. "He thought it made him look more trustworthy."

Dan buttoned his neon green doctor's coat and decided to let her comment pass. His main concern was to put young patients at ease, and he thought bright colors did that best. Of course, he had to admit the green was almost as bilious as Amy's dress at the wedding.

There she was again, intruding on his thoughts when he needed to concentrate on meeting new patients. And his poison oak was still tormenting him. Apparently, he'd missed a few spots, much to his distress.

"I've put Mrs. Johnson in room one," Georgia said. "Her chart is on the door. Poor thing can't seem to get her asthma under control. Of course, it's been a bad spring for allergies, but now that it's June, she should be feeling better. I suspect she's going to need steroids. Of course, she's afraid they'll make her gain weight."

"Check her blood pressure. I'll see her in a few minutes," Dan said, wondering why they needed him when nurses and pharmacists were so quick to prescribe.

"Done. She's one forty-two over eighty, but no doubt it will go down after you see her. She always gets nervous before she sees the doctor. And her weight is spot-on at 132. All that worry about gaining is mostly in her head."

Georgia's curls bounced around the edges of her nurse's cap. Dan couldn't remember the last time he'd seen such an old-fashioned uniform. She was starchy and white right down to her hose and sensible shoes.

In spite of the publicity about his arrival, Dan only had four patients, including a divorcee who wanted to talk to him about breast implants.

"It's not my field of expertise," he explained to the flashy redhead. "But I don't think the benefits justify the risk in your case."

By the time he'd said the same thing in six or seven different ways, he understood the value of a good nurse. Georgia burst into the examining room and cut short the consultation.

"That's it for today," the nurse said when the waiting room was empty. "Folks in Heart City are pretty healthy. Of course, people are used to going to the emergency room at the hospital or Bert Warner at the pharmacy."

"The pharmacist sees patients?" He was beginning to see how the town had gotten along without a doctor since the last one had retired.

"Oh, no, nothing like that. Folks just like to check with him or Amy before they waste time driving nearly twenty miles to see a doctor."

A bell on the door heralded the arrival of what could be a walk-in patient, so Georgia hustled out to the waiting room. After a few minutes, she came back to Dan's office, where he'd just finished smearing more ointment on the itching still tormenting him.

"Dr. Graham, this is Dr. Prince, straight from the University of Iowa Medical School," the portly nurse said in the tone of one introducing a favorite grandchild.

"Nice to meet you."

Dan found his hand in a vise-like grip, surprising in a man who barely came up to his chin and weighed less than the average twelve-year-old.

"My pleasure," Dan said, taking in the man's chartreuse and orange

Hawaiian shirt, baggy golf knickers, and knit cap with a stiff bill.

"I'll leave you two doctors to get acquainted," Georgia said with a serene smile.

"So how's it going?" Dr. Graham asked.

"This is my first day."

Dan didn't know whether the retired physician wanted a progress report or was only being courteous. Probably the latter, since he immediately launched into a long monologue about the best golf courses in the county.

"How long did you practice here?" Dan asked, genuinely curious.

"I came here planning to stay a year, got married, and stayed thirty-nine," the elderly man said without further comment.

"That's a long time," Dan said, not knowing what else to say.

"My wife and I have a condo in Florida," Dr. Graham said, "but she misses her friends here. So every spring we snowbirds make the trek back."

After nearly half an hour of aimless chatter, the retired physician got down to his excuse for being there.

"I left some old medical journals in the closet with the custodian's supplies. I got to thinking maybe I should take them home and see if there's anything worth keeping. I'll recycle what I don't want. Get them out of your way."

Before the old man finally left, Dan went from impatience to sympathy. The guy was bored out of his skin with retirement, and all he had to do today was drive his wife to her hair appointment. The old guy apparently had never intended to have a career in rural Iowa. Why hadn't he married the woman and taken her away with him? Dan shuddered, able to see himself in the retired physician's place, knocking a little ball around acres of grass when all he wanted to do was recapture his glory days of surfing in the Pacific.

Against his better judgment, he decided to grab a sandwich at the drug store lunch counter because it was convenient. Just because he was bored and, yes, a little lonely after leaving his many friends in Iowa City, it didn't mean he should take an interest in Amy. She probably wouldn't stand out at all on the university campus. He was only thinking about her because the prospects for any kind of diversion in the small town were nil.

The swivel stools at the soda fountain were filled, but Dan decided to wait. It was nearly one o'clock, and people would probably be leaving soon to get back to work. To kill time, he wandered the aisles, trying not to stare at the pharmacy department in the rear.

"Dr. Prince, how did your first day go?" Amy surprised him by appearing at the end of an aisle where she seemed to be recommending a pain relief cream to a mother with two kids in tow.

"Fine," he said, interested to see what she was up to.

She turned away from him to crouch and talk to a small boy around five or six who was sniffling and rubbing his eyes with grubby hands.

"This will make it feel better," she said, looking at his skinned knee. "But Mom has to wash it really well first so the dirty germs won't give you an infection."

Okay, Dan thought, she was clever about giving directions to the mother through her son. He certainly couldn't fault her for that.

While Amy finished with her customer, Dan wandered around the store, never losing sight of the pharmacist for more than a few moments. He thought of leaving to seek out a more appealing lunch, but she had him mesmerized. This morning he'd been annoyed by her advice, but she obviously had a compassionate nature. He'd overreacted, since she certainly wouldn't be prescribing for conditions requiring medical attention.

Clenching his fists to resist scratching a patch that still plagued him, he wandered back to the aisle with ointments, bandages, and such. He was tempted to try some over-the-counter meds, but his pride wouldn't let him. His prescription would work. He just had to be sure he hadn't overlooked any more spots, which was not easy when he was itching in places he couldn't see. He remembered taking his shirt off while he was working outside, apparently a bad decision.

At least he might as well have a sandwich. He found an empty stool and slid onto it, surprised to find himself sitting next to Amy.

"I have to warn you, the sandwiches are made and wrapped at the local deli," she said. "Some are pretty good, but if you get here at the end of the lunch rush, there's not much choice left."

A pert young woman who bounced up like a former cheerleader, which was probably what she was, came to take both their orders.

"Okay, guys, what will it be?"

"Josie, this is Dr. Prince," Amy said. "What sandwiches do you have left?"

"Ham and cheese on rye—I got a few complaints those were dry—and tuna salad. I think they have too much mayonnaise, but that's me," the counter worker said.

"I'll take a tuna," Amy said, "with my usual."

"Tuna and iced tea," Josie called out, although she was the only one working behind the counter. "What can I get for you, Dr. Prince?"

"I'll take a chance on ham and cheese with a frosted root beer," he said.

"Not a fan of tuna?" Amy teased.

"Fresh grilled is great. It's mayonnaise I don't much like." He couldn't imagine a more trivial conversation, but discussing it with her invested it with new meaning.

"I usually bring a sack lunch," Amy said, "but since I have my own apartment, it sometimes seems like too much nuisance to fix it. Guess my mom spoiled me with all those years of gourmet school lunches."

"My mother used to deliver my lunch to the elementary school," he said sheepishly. "Of course, when she got a full-time job, that had to stop. It was a little embarrassing anyway, but I loved the special treatment."

He couldn't remember ever telling that to anyone. What was it about this woman that coaxed memories like that from him?

The counter worker was right. His sandwich was so dry he was tempted to leave it, but instead he washed some of it down with root beer, an unusual beverage for him. The food was less important than the conversation. Amy had a way of making trivial subjects seem entertaining.

"I got an e-mail from my cousin—you know, the bride. Did you know Herbert Hoover was a great humanitarian? He was Iowa's only president. According to Mandy, he got a bum rap, getting saddled with The Great Depression. It wasn't the honeymoon report I'd expected."

"No, I wouldn't think so," he said, grinning at the couple's' choice of destination. Of course, if they'd never been any place, a presidential birthplace wasn't a terrible choice.

"I have to get back to work. Bert, my boss, won't be here until mid-afternoon. He had to go to his chiropractor in Des Moines. That's another profession we don't have here."

"Nice having lunch with you," Dan said, deciding to abandon the last section of sandwich. "And you were good with the little boy. I liked the way you instructed his mother indirectly."

"Hopefully it sunk in. She's not noted for smart decisions. She's on her fourth husband, and he's no improvement over the first three. But I don't want to bore you with small-town gossip."

She slid off the stool and started toward the back of the store.

He started to go after her, but stopped himself. What else could he say to her? They'd had lunch, and that was it. He was as determined as ever not to become involved with anyone in Heart City. Unlike the little retired doctor, he wasn't vulnerable to an infatuation that would determine the course of his life. If that meant avoiding Amy, it was a small price to pay for getting back to California where he belonged.

It was too bad she was lively, intelligent, and sexy, not to mention genuinely pretty. Two years was a long time to resist temptation.

CHAPTER 5

"The poor man has been here nearly two weeks. It's about time someone offered him some hospitality." Alice Crane tried to stare down her daughter, but Amy wasn't having it.

"No, no, no," Amy said. "Absolutely not. I know what you two are up to, and I'm not going along with it."

"How are you going to marry Prince Charming if you hide from him?" Hannah stared at her with saucer eyes, using all her seven-year-old charms trying to sway her aunt.

"You two are impossible," Amy said, shaking her head at her mother and niece. "For one thing, I don't cook—not when I can avoid it, anyway. Secondly, when a single woman invites an unmarried man to her apartment, it's a date, not hospitality. The last time I checked, the man was supposed to do the asking."

"Oh, dear," her mother said with a chuckle. "My grandmother was more progressive than you are. Haven't you heard it's okay to invite a gentleman to dinner?"

"I am not asking Dr. Prince to dinner at my place, no matter how much you two gang up on me," Amy said, throwing up her arms in mock despair.

"Don't you like him?" Hannah sounded genuinely distressed.

"Yes, he seems nice," Amy said to pacify her niece, although she actually did find the new doctor pleasant when he wasn't annoying her by questioning how she did her job.

"If your cooking is holding you back, I could help out," her mother suggested. "I've never met a man who didn't love my spare ribs—or maybe a nice pot roast with new potatoes and tiny onions would be better."

"No, Mom," Amy said.

"Of course, he's a doctor," she went on as though she hadn't heard her daughter's objections. "Maybe he thinks red meat isn't heart-healthy. I have a new recipe for tilapia . . . "

"No!" Amy said more emphatically.

"Now that I think of it, I could have a small dinner party at my house. I know your sister would love to come—and Mandy is home from her honeymoon."

"Invite her parents too. Aunt Linda could bring her ambrosia salad, and Uncle Pete is always good for a laugh when he tries to blow smoke rings with his pipe." Amy resorted to sarcasm, something she rarely did, since her mother seemed to be deaf to her protests.

"My friend Connie might like to come. She's been curious about the new doctor," her mother mused.

"Mom! I was kidding. Why would a complete stranger want to come to one of our family dinners?"

Amy slid out of the lounger on her mother's back deck, trying to think of a reason to leave. When she'd brought her laundry to do in her mother's washer and dryer, she hadn't expected to spend the waiting time fending off two rabid matchmakers.

"Does Dr. Prince have a mommy and daddy?" Hannah asked, as though the question had just occurred to her.

"He has a mother in California. Unfortunately his father passed away when he was very young," Amy said, recalling a conversation they'd had the last time he had lunch at the drug store.

"How sad," her mother said. "I didn't know that. Was it cancer?"

Amy was sorry she'd mentioned it. Even after more than ten years, her mother's sorrow for her deceased husband was still near the surface.

Shaking her head rather than discussing it in front of Hannah, Amy mouthed the words "auto accident."

"All the more reason to make him welcome here," her mother said, never one to give up easily when she started to imagine wedding bells for her daughter and more grandchildren for her.

Amy left as soon as she could, promising to return for her laundry later in the day. Her social calendar was the opposite of full, but she did have errands to run and her apartment to clean. She never knew what day she'd have off until Bert posted the work schedule on Monday morning, but this week Thursday was working well. Some weeks her boss wanted Tuesday off to go to his service club breakfast, although why he needed a full day to recover from it, she didn't know. More often, he took Saturday off, leaving her to run the store. At least they closed every day at six and never opened on Sundays or holidays, unlike pharmacies in larger towns. It was one of the perks she liked about working in Heart City.

As emphatic as she'd been about not inviting Dan to dinner at her apartment or her mother's house, she wasn't as indifferent as she pretended. He was on her mind as she hurried to the combination dry cleaners and commercial laundry to pick up her work jackets. Having them done there was a little luxury she allowed herself, since they turned out as limp as old rags when she did them herself.

"Hello, Pharmacist Amy." Dan startled her coming out the door as she was about to enter.

Her nose was only inches from one of his infamous neon lab coats. It took her a few moments to realize he'd just picked them up along with jeans in a plastic dry cleaners bag. No one could accuse him of being a conservative dresser. He stood out like a clown at a birthday party in the rural Iowa town.

"Oh, you have your laundry done here," she said, instantly realizing what a lame comment that was.

"Beats turning my shorts orange," he said. "I was going to call you."

She'd heard that before—usually from men who wanted to break up. Fortunately, he was so tall she didn't have to look directly into his penetrating brown eyes. No doubt if she did, he'd diagnose her discomfort about meeting him head-on. In fact, the more she saw of him, the more disconcerting their accidental meetings seemed. Some men undressed women with their eyes; Dan Prince seemed to look into her head. The last thing she wanted him to see there was the little crush she was trying to hide from everyone, especially him.

"How about having dinner with me tomorrow?" he asked, letting her slip by him into the dry cleaner's but following right behind.

"If you're free, that is," he said when surprise made her hesitate a moment.

"Yes, I think I am."

She knew exactly what was written on her calendar for Friday: nothing. Once in a while, she had a casual date, usually one set up by a friend, but the pickings were slim in Heart City. When she dreamed about finding a soul mate, it usually involved going on vacation somewhere exotic. In fact, she'd been saving up for a Mediterranean cruise sometime in the far future.

"Great." He said it matter-of-factly. Did he realize no woman in town would say no to him, unconventional as he was as a doctor garbed in neon and jeans?

"I work until six." She didn't know whether to hope it was too late for him. "If you're hungry and want to eat earlier . . . "

"Will it rush you if I come by for you at seven?"

"No, I don't live far from the store."

In fact, she had a cozy studio apartment in what had once been a warehouse. A local realtor had converted it into two floors of rental units after it sat empty for years. Amy loved the colorful metal awnings shading small individual balconies with a view of Johnson Creek and rolling farmland. One of the perks of Heart City was no one had to go far for pretty scenery.

"In the apartment building with red and white awnings, right?"

"Yes. How do you know?" She certainly didn't remember telling him. In fact, she had a clear recollection of every conversation they'd had. There hadn't been that many.

"Don't you know a physician has to be a good investigator?" he teased.

"Georgia Stewart must have told you. I heard she's working for you," Amy said.

"I thought I was working for her," he said with the light laugh she enjoyed. "But she is a font of information. I have to run, but I'll see you tomorrow at seven."

Well, she had a date, sort of. Her mother would be thrilled, and Hannah would launch into her Prince Charming scenario when she told them—if she told them. Maybe it would be better to let the news filter back to them through Heart City's all too reliable tell-a-person line. It was quicker than posting on Facebook, and at least she wouldn't have to make lengthy explanations about how they were only casual friends.

She started to regret saying yes almost immediately. Sure, the new doctor had heart-stopping good looks and the potential to be a really hot date, but warning signs popped up in her head whenever she was near him.

Falling in love with Dan would be easy to do, given his obvious charm, but would surely lead to heartbreak. Nothing could possibly come of becoming attached to the newcomer. He only wanted to pass the time of day with her while he fulfilled his obligation in Heart City. She would only be his temporary cure for boredom.

It was too late to say no this time, but she vowed to avoid him in the future.

*

Asking Amy to dinner had seemed like a good idea when Dan woke up that morning. His practice kept him busy enough in the daytime, but his evenings already seemed long and dull. He'd seen the only movie playing in town, watched baseball teams he didn't care about on TV, and gingerly worked to get rid of the poison oak behind his apartment. A man could only spend so much time running, reading, and daydreaming about the possibility of joining a lucrative clinic in California.

Now that he'd taken the plunge and asked her out, he had

reservations. He was working on the saturation principle. If he saw more of her, she wouldn't seem as beguiling. They probably had nothing in common, and the little spark between them would diminish with familiarity.

Yeah, that was his theory, and he was stuck with it, at least through tomorrow's dinner date. He wasn't looking forward to testing his theory as much as he'd anticipated. What if the date was great and they had a real connection? He didn't want another failed romance, and it wasn't his intention to hurt Amy.

No matter how it went tomorrow evening, this had to be a one date deal. He went back to his office thinking about the retired doctor in his sad golfing garb. Dr. Graham was a perfect example of what small-town life did to an otherwise intelligent man. Love had been his snare, but Dan wasn't going to step into that trap. As delightful as Amy seemed to be, she would never play a part in his plans for the future.

CHAPTER 6

When his cell phone rang, Dan was already running late for his date with Amy. He was tempted to ignore it and leave, but he had responsibilities now. It might be a potential patient or a summons to an accident site. Everyone who could possibly have need of his services had his personal number, including the head of the hospital, the police chief, the county sheriff, and even school and day care administrators.

He checked caller I.D. and smiled.

"Hello, this is Dr. Dan, uncle of the infamous Prince boys of Sacramento," he said, pleased to get a call from his only sibling.

"You're silly, Uncle Dan," his eight-year-old nephew Tray giggled.

"I got it from your father. He tickled me too much when we were kids," Dan teased. "What's going on at your house?"

"Tony hit a home run," his younger nephew reported.

"I wanted to tell him," his nine-year-old brother said, grabbing the phone away from Tray.

Dan perched on a kitchen chair and enjoyed a lengthy account of his nephew's Little League triumph until his father confiscated the phone.

"How's it going in the Heartland?" Greg asked.

His brother was seven years older and the father of two boys and a third on the way. One of the things Dan wanted to do was find a way to help Greg's family when he was practicing in California. Greg taught high school science, and it was a struggle to raise a family on his salary, even with his wife Ginny's help as a substitute teacher. The unplanned pregnancy was putting an even greater strain on their finances, but Dan envied his brother's love of teaching. Would he ever love medicine that much? He had high hopes, but was bogged down paying off his obligation to Heart City.

"I visited two day care centers today," Dan said. "Wanted the little ones to see me informally in my lab coat before they have a visit at the office. I let them listen to their own hearts. It was fun."

"You should be an elementary teacher," Greg teased. "Kids love you."

"Sounds like a good way to starve."

Dan checked his watch and realized he had only minutes to get to Amy's apartment on time. Still, it was great to hear from his brother, and he wanted an update on all that was happening in his life. For years, it had only been the three of them, Greg, their mother, and him. He wondered if he'd ever feel as close to a woman as he did to his family. Although he'd never made definite plans for their future, he was still soured on romance.

"I have to go," he said when it was past time to pick up his date.

"I'm sorry about Belinda," his brother said.

"Yeah, who knew she was only interested in a doctor with a lucrative California practice?" Dan said with a trace of bitterness.

"Well, better to find out now," Greg said philosophically. "Have you met anyone in—what's the name of that town again?"

"Heart City. No, the last thing I need is a woman who might want to tie me down here. I can't wait to finish my two years and get on with my life."

"You've only just begun," his older brother said. "Maybe you'll end up loving it there."

Dan laughed in response. "My biggest hope is I've eradicated all the poison oak in back of my apartment. I still itch when I think about the case I contracted. Keep me posted on the baby."

"Will do," Greg said, signing off.

Dan checked his watch again. After a nice long conversation with his brother, he was twenty minutes late and counting. He'd have to drive, even though her apartment was within walking distance. In fact, everything in town was easy to reach on foot, but he didn't think much of guys who showed up late for dates. Rushing out to his car, he was surprised at how eager he was to see her.

*

He's a doctor, Amy told herself. There were all kinds of emergencies that may have made him late. Letting her imagination run wild didn't push away the other possibilities: He'd changed his mind or had simply forgotten their date.

Why was she wearing her newest, cutest dress, a little yellow number with a short bouncy skirt? If she were being stood up, she'd only feel worse because she'd dressed up. Dan was nearly half an hour late, and he hadn't even bothered to call. She knew because she'd been carrying her phone around with her the last fifteen minutes. He could at least have the courtesy to let her know if he wasn't coming.

Just when she'd decided to change into shorts and an old tank top, her doorbell rang.

Counting slowly to twenty so she wouldn't seem eager, she made her leisurely way to the door. This wasn't an important date, and she was going to play it cool no matter what his reason was for being late.

"No excuse," Dan said with a sheepish grin when she opened the door.

"Oh, are you late?" She feigned indifference but it was hard to pull off while wearing three-inch heels that didn't compensate for their height difference.

"A little," he said, raising one dark eyebrow in skepticism.

"Okay, you're thirty two and a half minutes late, but I'm sure you have a good reason." She only wanted to get the evening over with, so there was no point in playing games.

"My brother called just as I was leaving. We hadn't talked in quite a while. Afraid I lost track of time. He's expecting his third son pretty soon."

He rattled off his reasons, at least giving her some fodder for their dinner conversation. She really didn't know much about him, other than that he was only in Heart City for two years.

Her feet hurt already from pacing around her apartment, so she breathed a sigh of relief when she saw he'd brought his van. It was only six blocks or so to the town's best eatery, but keeping up with his long strides would be like trying to catch a guy on stilts. The sad truth was that he wasn't her size, shape, or type. It was a darn shame he was the living image of a Greek god, but looks weren't everything.

Friday night meant dinner out for everyone under fifty. The local restaurants ran senior-citizen specials on Tuesday and Thursday to make room for the family trade on Fridays and date nights on Saturday. Of course, Dan didn't know the Knife and Fork would be packed with big groups gathered around tables pushed together to accommodate their numbers.

"Looks pretty busy," he commented unnecessarily as they waited in line to leave their names with the hostess.

"Friday is like one big family reunion," she said, shuddering as she remembered her mother's plan to invite him to a dinner with all their relatives.

"People here hardly ever get sitters," she said. "They just bring the kids along. It was slim pickings back in the days when I was trying to earn spending money by babysitting."

"That's nice, really," Dan said thoughtfully. "I imagine working mothers want their kids nearby in the evening."

"We can squeeze you into the back room if you don't mind being a little crowded," the young, pink-faced hostess said, flicking aside her long head-hugging helmet of red hair.

Why on earth was the girl wearing high heels and a black cocktail dress to seat people at the Knife and Fork? Amy could imagine how much her feet must hurt at the end of the evening.

And why was she starting to think like the self-proclaimed spinster who lived across from her mother? Had her youth faded away now that she had a professional degree and a job where she wore a white coat?

"That'll be great," Dan said, handing the young hostess a folded bill.

"You don't have to tip her," Amy whispered in the softest possible voice as they followed the hostess to a rear room sometimes used for wedding receptions. "No one does."

"She'll need to save up for a podiatrist," he whispered back, leaning down to speak close to her ear.

His breath tickled her ear, and she totally forgot about the hostess as they walked into a room with a noise level only slightly below a rock concert.

"I think they'll be having dessert soon," the hostess said as Amy picked her way over a snowstorm of breadcrumbs. Apparently, the rowdy youngsters at the big table had found a way to entertain themselves while they waited for their orders.

Pulling out a chair for her, Dan impressed her with courtesy. The man certainly knew how to treat a date, even though they had to shout at each other to be heard over the lively party dominating the room.

"Would you like to go somewhere else?" Amy asked, leaning close to be heard.

Maybe he was the one who should suggest it, but she was embarrassed by the rowdy group. She didn't want him to think the town was overrun by ill-mannered people who paid no attention to their children's bad behavior.

Dan shook his head. "The kids are a hoot. They're doing what every kid wants to do at a stuffy adult dinner."

Hiding her surprise, she realized he was right. She could remember endless dinners when her great aunt visited. The staid older woman, who'd never had children herself, insisted Amy and Natalie sit at the table until she finished eating her meal in tiny bites. It was agonizing to watch her consume a meal in slow motion, and the two of them often fell into giggling fits before their mother finally excused them from the table.

"All they need is someone to play quiet table games with them," Dan said, sounding wistful. "According to my brother, our dad was a whiz at making them up. Of course, I don't remember."

"What does your brother do now?" she asked, genuinely curious because Dan's face had lit up with he mentioned the phone call.

"Teaches high school science." His features softened, and she could tell he was genuinely fond of his brother.

Service was slow, but Amy was fascinated by Dan's memories of growing up with a widowed mother.

"I never would've become a doctor without her encouragement," Dan said. "She worked her way up from a temp job to a museum curator's secretary, so I figured I could get through med school one way or another. At the time, I thought help from Heart City was a miracle."

"And now?" She wasn't sure she wanted to know the answer.

"Two years seem like a long time. I'm eager to get back to California and get settled for good."

She knew that already, but the way he said it touched her heart. It couldn't be easy to hit a roadblock after so many years of work and study. The best she could hope was that the town would appreciate his work the way they should.

"Dr. Prince?"

A dark-haired woman Amy knew by sight as a customer at the drug store stood beside their table with a little girl who mirrored her mother's good looks.

"Yes." Dan's smile melted Amy's heart, and she knew she was in danger of caring about him too much.

"Jennie met you at the day care today. She wanted to give you her cookie to thank you for coming."

An engaging little girl about four years old held out a big, round frosted cookie, a specialty of the restaurant.

"It was her own idea," the mother said as Dan took it.

"Thank you, Jennie. This is so kind of you," he said with a winning smile. He took a bite and chewed with gusto. He couldn't have been more charming if the president's wife had presented him with a medal. "You drew that pretty picture of the flowers in your garden."

The little girl was beaming as her mother led her away. "You remembered her drawing?" Amy said in awe. Doctors had to be smart, but how could he recall one child's picture in a room full of kids?

"I have to confess," he said grinning. "All the children were drawing flowers."

"Well, you've made a fan for life—for as long as you're here."

"It's hard to treat children when you have to hurt them to do it," he said thoughtfully. "I don't want them to be afraid of me, so I'll probably visit elementary classrooms when school starts."

"That's a wonderful idea if you have time," she said.

"I'll make time," he said in a determined voice.

The meal wasn't memorable. Her lamb chops were dry, and the medley of garden vegetables was steam-table limp. Dan didn't mention his grilled fish, but he spent a lot of time extracting little bones. If the success of the evening depended on the food, it was a flop.

Instead, her heart was singing as they walked to his van. Dan was fun. He loved to tease, but there was no meanness in it. Even though he didn't want to be in Heart City, he seemed to like the people, especially the young children he'd gone out of his way to meet.

"What do we do for an encore?" he asked, opening the door of the van for her. "We can make the nine o'clock movie."

"There's only a fifty-fifty chance the projector will be working," she said, a little embarrassed by the lack of a good movie theater. The antiquated Cinema Palace was more a hobby than a viable business for the owners, a semi-retired couple known to have inherited a fortune from a bachelor uncle.

"I thought it was a little jerky when I went to a Schwarzenegger rerun last week. Classy theater, though. I love the effect of a starlit sky and the fake balconies."

"It's been renovated since I was a kid. Now all they need is a major technological update and some first-run movies. Of course, now you can see almost anything on DVDs," she said.

"I have a copy of *True Grit*, the John Wayne version, I haven't seen. My brother gave it to me for my birthday."

Amy wrinkled her nose, but not at his brother's taste in movies. Watching a movie in his apartment seemed a little too cozy for a first date that couldn't possibly go anywhere.

"If you want to get a true taste of Iowa, let's go to the gravel pit," she suggested, tongue in cheek.

"A gravel pit?" For once, he looked totally puzzled. "Do we look for fossils or something?"

"Not unless you're into diving. There aren't many natural lakes in Iowa, at least not around here. Local kids swim in a flooded gravel pit. The parking area is sort of a hang-out too, but not this early in the evening."

"I'm game," he said in a teasing voice, "so long as the new doctor doesn't get arrested for skinny dipping."

"Believe me, that's not going to happen!"

She slipped out of her shoes as soon as she was belted in, wiggling her toes in relief. As soon as she got home, they were going in her charity bag. Why torture her feet for a date that was going nowhere?

Dan followed her directions through a twisting maze of back roads and parked in a level area east of the gravel pit. As expected, the young crowd wasn't there yet, which made it a pleasant place to watch the sunset.

Gorgeous shades of orange and pink streaked the western sky as Dan came around to her side of the car, catching her with her feet bare.

"I thought we could walk a little, but if your feet hurt . . ."

"Oh, no, I'm fine," she lied, not wanting to seem like a silly female who wore uncomfortable shoes. She slipped her protesting feet into the too-high heels and took his hand to get out of the van.

Two steps away, she stepped into a depression in the uneven ground and stumbled, saved from a fall by his quick reflexes. His arm shot out to catch her, and she ended up with her face pressed against the soft cotton knit on his chest.

"Sorry," she stammered, unhurt but embarrassed.

"Take my arm," he said, dismissing it so casually she felt at ease immediately. "I can see why you brought me here. I really miss the sunsets over the Pacific."

For the briefest of moments, he sounded like a homesick boy. Then he laughed at his own flash of nostalgia and led her to the waterside.

"Kids swim here?" he asked, more in wonder than doubt.

"The big ones do. There's no lifeguard, so they do it at their own risk. No one's ever drowned, but there've been some bruises and breaks when kids get rowdy."

"Is this where you went when you were a kid?" he asked, keeping a tight grip on her hand.

"Sometimes. New cheerleaders had to skinny dip before they were considered part of the squad. It sounds raunchy, but once you're in the water, it's—I don't know how to describe it."

"Sensual," he purred in a voice so low she might have mistaken the word. "I don't suppose . . ."

"No."

"Bad idea. I apologize for even thinking it," he said, not sounding the least bit sorry.

The air was cool after a long, hot day, and Amy wasn't sorry for bringing him here, even though she may have sent him the wrong message. It seemed a long time since she'd held hands with a boy at the edge of the gravel pit. Maybe it wasn't romantic by anyone else's standards, but the solitude and the quiet in the surrounding woods gave the setting a special charm.

Dan was quiet, but she suspected he wasn't thinking about her. Only Hannah believed Prince Charming would come into her life and transform it into the stuff of fairy tales.

"I guess we should go and leave the place to the kids," he said when only a sliver of the great orange ball still showed on the horizon. "Don't want to cramp their style."

The parking area was darker and more treacherous, but he led her back to the van without incident. They didn't seem to have much to talk about on the way back to town, or maybe he was as lost in thought as she was.

When he parked by her apartment building, she quickly got out of the vehicle, ready to end the evening as smoothly as possible. This was probably their first and only date, and she didn't want him to think she expected more.

"I can make it from here," she said with an unintended giggle.

"I don't know how they do it in Iowa, but we California men see a lady to her door."

He hurried to take her arm, perhaps concerned she might take a header in her heels, but she'd taken the precaution of dangling them from her hand. A little rough cement on her soles was preferable to skinned knees or worse.

"This is what I call the awkward moment," he said when they were standing outside her door. "A kiss is called for, but may not be welcome. On the other hand, it has connotations neither party might not welcome."

"What are you talking about?" she teased to cover her own discomfort.

Of course, she wanted him to kiss her. Little girls too young for kindergarten courted his attention, and she was, after all, a warm-blooded female. But locked lips could lead to complications. She didn't want him to think she was a predatory female out to snare the town's hunky new doctor. A little pride wasn't a bad thing.

"Thank you for the dinner," she said in a deliberately formal tone.

"My pleasure. Thank you for sharing your lover's lane with me. I enjoyed watching the sunset with you."

Lover's lane? What an old-fashioned expression. Before she could comment on it, he bent his head and planted a soft kiss on her forehead.

"Good night, Amy."

He'd kissed her forehead. She unlocked the door and quickly

closed it behind her. What kind of message did a kiss on the forehead send? One thing was sure: It was about as romantic as shaking hands.

The evening had been fun. She'd had a good time, and that was that. The less she saw of Dr. Dan Prince in the future, the safer she'd feel. If she allowed herself to have any expectations about him, she was open to heartache.

Her forehead still tingled where his lips had touched it. She rubbed the spot, as though she could erase the memory of his kiss. The sooner she put him totally out of her mind, the better it would be for her.

CHAPTER 7

"What are you compounding?"

Amy watched with curiosity Monday afternoon as Bert Warner vigorously ground a mix of dry ingredients. Pharmacists rarely had to use a mortar and pestle these days when every imaginable remedy came pre-packaged.

"It's my secret horse liniment. I'm mixing it for Gil Brown. His favorite horse, Briny, has gone lame, and he swears by it."

"What's in it?" Amy wrinkled her nose at the pungent odor, only made worse when he added a huge dollop of a greasy substance.

"Ah, that's a secret I won't part with until I'm retired for good," he said, his voice teasing but his expression earnest.

"Not even to your number one pharmacist?" Amy asked with a grin.

It was a running joke because she was his only professional employee. Until he hired her, Bert had worked long hours without another pharmacist. He still had the husky build of a University of Iowa linebacker, but he admitted his knees weren't what they'd once been. If their working relationship continued to be as congenial as it was now, Bert planned to gradually reduce his hours. Amy knew he hoped to make it possible for her to buy the store eventually, although his full retirement was still some time in the future.

"The formula is locked away with my will. It goes to the person who takes over the store." He added another ingredient and pounded vigorously.

Amy thought he must be kidding, but his expression belied that. Bert was as serious about his concoction as Gil Brown was about the horses he bred.

"Would you mind running this out to Gil's place?" Bert asked. "My car is in the shop, and my wife is visiting her sister in

Dubuque with hers."

"Sure, no trouble," Amy said.

Bert was her ideal boss, always requesting she do things instead of giving orders. He was one of the reasons she liked her job so much and appreciated the pace of life in Heart City.

"Better leave as soon as I get this ready," he said. "We're under a tornado watch, but you should have plenty of time before it turns into a warning—if it does."

"No problem. I'm an Iowa girl, you know."

Amy had learned in kindergarten how to take cover from a tornado, and she still knew exactly where to go when a warning was issued. She'd only rented her apartment after she was sure there was easy access to a cellar.

While Bert scooped the liniment into an empty plastic jar, she grabbed her purse and got ready to go. The Brown farm was seven or eight miles from town, but she knew the way because Gil's daughter Gayle had been her friend all the way through school.

"I'll put this on Gil's account," Bert said, handing her the bag containing his remedy. "Hurry back before the storm gets here."

"Sure thing, Pops," she said, smiling at his concern. Sometimes he did sound like a father, which, of course, he was. But his only son had chosen the military over pharmacy, a major disappointment to Bert since the drug store wouldn't stay in the Warner family.

Although she wouldn't mention it to her boss, Amy was grateful to leave for a while. Every other customer was curious about her date with Dan. In fact, some invented excuses for their trip to the store, asking bogus questions in hopes of getting details about her dinner with the doctor.

Josie was the worst of all. Even when she wasn't asking questions, she gave Amy snide little grins, as though she were privy to some great secret.

"The doctor and I are not an item," she'd emphatically told her friend, but she might as well protest to a brick wall.

Of course, she wasn't naive. People had waited a long time for a resident doctor, and they didn't want him to leave after two years. What better way to ensure he stayed than to pair him with a local woman? What no one realized was that prying eyes and gossip only drove a bigger wedge between them. Amy wouldn't feel comfortable saying hello to him on the street with so much attention focused on their nonexistent relationship.

"By the time you get back, it will be nearly closing time," Bert said as she was leaving. "Take the rest of the afternoon off. I'll lock up."

"Thanks, Bert," she said, happy to make the delivery.

In fact, she was glad to leave the public eye and have some time alone with her thoughts. She didn't try to kid herself. Dan was the first really interesting man she'd met since leaving college, and it wouldn't be hard to become enamored of him. She already had a little crush on the doctor, but then, what woman wouldn't find him special? He was sexy without flaunting it, the most dangerous kind of sensuality. Not only that, he was kind, an underrated attribute, but one she prized.

Obviously she couldn't spend two years avoiding him in a town as small of Heart City, but she absolutely could not let their friendship develop into anything more: no more dates, no more sunsets at the gravel pit, and no more chaste little kisses on her forehead that left her yearning for more.

"That's settled," she said aloud as she turned off the county road on her way to Gil Brown's farm. "Dr. Prince can find someone else to kill time with."

*

Dan marveled at the variety of services he was called upon to perform in the small town. The last thing he'd expected was to fill in for the town's only large animal vet. He'd met Dr. George Granger, a robust fifty-year-old, at a service club lunch where he'd been invited to meet the town's leaders. Now he found himself trying to find a farm out in the boonies to look at a horse with a bum leg.

Of course, Dr. Granger didn't expect him to diagnose animal ailments while he was enjoying a rare vacation in Las Vegas. But apparently Gil Brown was a friend as well as a horse breeder, someone he couldn't put off when he got an urgent call in his Vegas hotel room.

"I really appreciate this," the vet had said on the phone to Dan after giving him detailed instructions about applying a compress to the horse's injured leg. "Gil knows almost as much as I do about his mare's problems, but it will ease his mind to have a medical man check it out. There's some bad blood between him and the vet who stands in for me, so I really owe you one on this."

After Dan processed what he'd been asked to do, he was actually excited about his visit to the horse farm. As an undergraduate, a friend at school had invited him home for the winter break since it was too far—and too expensive—to go to California. It was a mild December for Iowa, and Dan had learned to ride one of the farm family's horses. He was a little intimidated about working with one now, but at least he wasn't a complete stranger to an animal that large.

Fortunately, Granger's directions to the farm weren't too difficult to follow, although the countryside was still a maze in Dan's mind. The sky was overcast, and in his eyes threatening, but the call shouldn't take long. Hopefully he could get back to town before a storm broke.

He turned onto a long gravel driveway leading to a complex of buildings, the largest of which was a long metal stable that looked nothing like the traditional red barns in calendar art.

As he pulled into a parking area, he had a rude surprise. Unless he was very much mistaken, the small blue compact car beside his van was Amy's. What was the pharmacist doing on a horse farm?

Hurrying toward the open door of the stable, he was as annoyed as he was puzzled. He could clearly hear her voice and a low-pitched male's, so he didn't hesitate to approach them, scarcely noticing the stalls or their occupants as he went to the far end of the building.

"What on earth?" The scene in front of him sucked away his breath, and he hardly knew how to react.

A man in dirty jeans and a faded plaid shirt was stooped over beside a fidgeting brown horse while Amy held the animal's bridle and stroked its head.

"Dr. Granger sent me," Dan said to explain his presence, not able to take his eyes off the pharmacist.

The horse breeder stood and wiped his fingers on a rag he pulled from his pocket. "You're a little late," the man said without introducing himself.

"Gil, this is Dr. Prince," Amy said, still focused on the horse.

"I have instructions from the vet. He thought you needed some help," Dan said, only acknowledging her with a nod.

"I'm obliged to you for coming," the lean, weathered older man said, "but Amy brought me some of Bert's special liniment. I think Briny will be okay now."

Dan's shoulders slumped, and he was too dumbfounded to speak. Not only did the town's pharmacists recommend over-the-counter cures for adults, they dabbled in veterinary medicine. He gave Amy a look that was meant to be withering, but she didn't even notice.

"It's Bert's secret formula," she explained without sounding the least bit intimidated by his stare.

The horse stood quietly, maybe reacting to the quiet hum of her voice, but Dan grew more annoyed as the man gave full attention to his animal.

"I have the supplies you need to treat your horse and instructions on how to use them," Dan said, not willing to leave until he'd fulfilled his promise to the vet.

"As I said," the man said without standing, "I have Bert Warner's liniment. It's worked in the past, and I see no reason why it won't do the job now, seeing as Granger is off goofing around in Vegas."

"Everyone needs a vacation." Dan had no idea why he was defending a vet he scarcely knew, but the farmer's attitude was off-putting.

"Don't want to tell you your business, but a storm is coming. Might even kick up a few tornadoes. You might want to get back to town before it hits," Gil Brown said. "You too, Amy."

"I'll leave this stuff here," Dan said, hoping he didn't sound as petulant as he felt. He was willing to do favors, but he didn't like being dismissed like an errand boy.

As he hurried out to his van, he was aware of Amy following close behind him.

"I'm not the one who concocted the liniment," she said defensively. "Anyway, people here have to be self-reliant. We can't depend on outsiders to come in and provide services."

"Is that how you think of me, as an outsider?" he asked, spinning around to confront her.

"No—well, yes, in some ways. You don't want to be here. You'll leave as soon as you can. How else should I think of you?"

"I guess it really doesn't matter." This was the dumbest quarrel he'd ever had. He'd wasted his time coming here, and nothing she could say would change that.

Her hair was blowing in her face, and her starched jacket billowed around her in the wind. Fine sand and debris pelted his face as he stepped into it. The horse breeder was right about one thing: It was time to head back to civilization, or what passed for it in Heart City. At least there were tornado shelters there. He didn't want to experience his first one out in open farmland.

"We'd better get moving. If you do spot a funnel cloud, leave the van and take cover in a ditch. Don't try to shelter in the underpass on the county road. A tornado will suck you out of there in a heartbeat." Amy opened the door of her little car, and the wind grabbed it out of her hand and nearly slammed it shut.

"Maybe you should ride with me," he said urgently. "My van

has more weight."

"Didn't you see the news report on the tornado that tossed around semi-trailers? Chances are we won't get hit, but it's time to get going," she said in a no-nonsense voice, forcing open her car door and climbing in.

She was the first to pull away, but he followed close behind. It was easier to follow her than to try reading the vet's directions in reverse, and Dan was edgy about the roaring wind and threat of worse to come.

Finding a clear station on the cheap radio in his van was harder than keeping his eye on Amy's car as she drove much too fast for his comfort. Either she was overly confident on the narrow roads, or she was really worried about a tornado. Either way, he was frightened by her speed and frustrated because he didn't know what to do to keep her safe if a storm did hit.

It was the longest ride of his life, much worse than rush hour traffic in Santa Barbara. Ahead of him, Amy took a curve like a NASCAR driver, and his heart was in his throat as he agonized over her safety. The only good thing was the lack of traffic. Apparently, all the sensible people in the area had hunkered down in safe places.

Finally, she pulled into town and headed toward her apartment building. He followed without giving it any thought, still concerned for her safety. When she parked, he pulled up beside her.

"You didn't need to follow me home," she said, getting out of her car and stepping up to the open window on the driver's side of the van.

"I just wanted to be sure you got here okay," he said, getting out of his vehicle.

"Well, as you can see, I did." Her tone was dismissive.

Thunder rumbled and lightning crackled too close for his comfort.

"We'd better get inside. Come on." She grabbed his hand and pulled with more force than he could've imagined coming from such a small woman. "There's a tornado warning. I heard it on my car radio."

Once inside the main entrance, she turned left and led him to a closed door, opening it and leading him down steep stairs lit by flickering lights.

"Darn, the landlord promised to install a generator—sometime in this century," she said, warning him to hold onto the railing if the power went out.

The murmur of voices told him they weren't the only ones seeking shelter in the basement. She led the way to a surprisingly pleasant recreation area with a ping pong table and a scattering of couches and chairs. A small group was gathered around a TV, watching the weather for their area.

"Amy, glad you made it," an older woman with thick glasses and yellowish hair said. "We're under a tornado warning."

As soon as she spoke, the power went out, plunging the room into utter and complete darkness. Dan reached for Amy's hand, and again she led him, this time to an unoccupied couch near where they stood. He sat down beside her, still clutching her hand.

"Guess we'll have to wait it out in the dark," an elderly man's voice said.

"I told you to grab the flashlight," a woman said.

"No, you told me to move my sorry behind if I didn't want it hanging from the top of the water tower," he retorted.

The older couple's argument would've been funny to Dan if he hadn't been sitting in pitch dark wondering if a tornado was going to demolish the town.

"How do you put up with the threat of tornados?" he asked, realizing his hand was interlocked with Amy's.

"How do people in California cope with the threat of earthquakes?" she asked, sounding peeved but not pulling her hand away.

"Good point," he had to admit, giving her hand what he hoped was a reassuring squeeze.

The room was silent, people intent on hearing the storm, although the sounds from outside were muffled.

"How much longer do you think?" the same elderly male voice asked.

"The weather said it should pass by four thirty. What time do you think it is?"

Remembering the watch on his wrist, Dan turned it so he could see the luminous numerals. "I have seventeen minutes after four."

"Did I remember to turn off the oven?" another voice asked. "I'd hate to have my pie ruined."

"How can it burn if the power is off?" a reedy voice asked.

Dan wasn't sure how many people were waiting out the storm in the cellar of the apartment building, but he hoped the whole town had taken shelter. He couldn't even imagine the number of injuries if a tornado caught people unaware. It was one thing to see a tragedy like that on TV, but another thing entirely when he was the only doctor in town.

"Do you think everyone made it to a shelter?" he quietly asked Amy.

"Yes, I'm sure they heard the siren in plenty of time," she assured him.

"Was that the siren I heard last week?"

"Yes, they test it every Thursday around supper time during the season. Nobody would ignore it any other time."

"That's good to know." He concentrated on reviewing his crisis management training in his head. No doctor could graduate these days without a crash course in emergency procedures. He felt bowled over by the possibility of being the only physician on the scene right after a disaster. It took the practice of medicine far beyond sore throats and sniffles.

"Can I have my hand back?" she whispered close to his ear.

"Sorry." He released it immediately, embarrassed by the way he'd clutched it.

"You know, I'm not the one who has a secret formula for horse liniment," she said after long moments of silence, keeping her voice low. "I was just the delivery girl."

"Sorry if I overreacted," he said contritely. "I'd never heard of a pharmacist who treats horses."

"Bert doesn't diagnose them. Gil Brown knows as much about horses as a vet. He loves them and treats them like his children. Years ago, he had a situation, and Bert concocted a salve that seemed to help. As far as I know, Gil is the only one who's ever used it—or even knows about it."

"I see." Actually, he did understand why a small community had to be inventive about solving problems. He just hoped neither of the pharmacists was suggesting medicines to people who needed to see a physician.

The lights came on, with sighs of relief all around the room. Now that he could see, he only had eyes for Amy. She was snuggled in the corner of the old flowery couch, her legs tucked up and her arms across her chest looking younger and more vulnerable than he knew her to be.

"You okay?" he asked.

"Fine." She was focused on the TV where the area weather station gave an all clear for Heart City and the surrounding area.

"I guess we can go," Dan said, finding he wasn't all that eager to leave her.

"Yes, we can." She was the first to move toward the stairs.

"Thanks," he said.

Turning to look back at him, she asked, "What for?"

"Bringing me down here." He shrugged, wishing she'd ask him up to her apartment, although there was no good reason to spend more time with her.

She hurried up the stairs to her second floor apartment without another word.

With no other choice, he dashed out to the van through the

downpour battering the town. Thankfully, he wouldn't have to treat disaster victims, but he was still disturbed by one fear: He might not be up to the responsibility of taking care of a town full of badly injured people. What would Heart City do if a tornado did strike and no physician was on the scene to give emergency care? It was a sobering thought, one he was sure would haunt his dreams.

CHAPTER 8

When she reached her apartment, Amy was still shaky, although it wasn't like her to be frightened by a tornado warning. Was it waiting out the threat in the dark basement or something entirely different that left her shivering like a wet cat?

Peeling off her damp clothes, she stepped into a warm shower, letting water cascade over her until she started to feel calm. By the time she was wrapped up in her thick terrycloth robe, nestled on the couch with a cup of tea, she was ready to admit the real cause of her agitation: Dan.

For someone who didn't want to be in Heart City, he was much too prickly about the way folks did things in her town. He'd glared at her because Gil Brown was using Bert's liniment, and she'd only made the delivery. What did a people-doctor know about taking care of horses? He was nothing but Dr. Granger's delivery boy himself.

When the phone rang, she had a moment of illogical hope, wondering if the doctor was calling to apologize for his judgmental attitude at the farm. Fat chance! It was her mother calling to be sure she'd gotten home all right.

"Did you have to go into the basement at the store?" she asked, knowing Amy didn't like the creepy old cellar.

Not that she was afraid, exactly, but a series of former owners over the last hundred years had left shelves crammed with outdated medicines, store displays, and oddities in the dungeon-like space. The ceiling was low with bare rafters festooned with cobwebs, and the two bare light bulbs at either end of the long space hardly gave enough light to walk through the rows. At the far end was an antiquated machine that had baled scrap paper a century before recycling became a buzz word. It reminded Amy of a guillotine. If she ever owned the store, she was going to have a junk dealer strip the cellar bare, but that was a long time in the future.

"No, I sat it out in the basement of my building. Bert had me make a delivery, then let me come home early. What about you?"

"Judge Barnum adjourned court at noon, but a bunch of us had to take cover in the basement of the courthouse."

"That's not so bad then," Amy said, a little disappointed in herself because she hadn't called to check on her mother. The high wind could've caused damage in town even without a funnel cloud.

At least her mother, a court clerk, worked in the most secure building in town, the Georgian-style county courthouse with massive pillars in front and thick walls.

"I've been thinking," her mother said in a solemn voice. "It's really a shame we haven't done anything to welcome the new doctor. I went to see him Friday . . . "

"As a patient?" Amy was quick to ask.

"Yes, of course, not that I'm sick or anything. I just had a quick appointment during my lunch break. I needed him to renew my allergy medicine before hay fever season."

"Which is at least a month away," Amy pointed out. "I thought the non-prescription pills were working fine."

"Yes, if the pollen count doesn't get too high. It never hurts to have something stronger in the house." Did her mother sound a little guilty?

"Did he prescribe what you wanted?" Amy asked, not hiding her skepticism. Her mother's hay fever was mild, especially since she spent most of her summer days in air conditioning.

"Not exactly. He suggested the pills I'm already using."

"You paid for an appointment to find out what I'd already told you?"

"It's good to establish a doctor-patient relationship before something goes seriously wrong," her mother said, a weak excuse if Amy had ever heard one.

"Why did you really see him?"

"I told you."

"You're trying to play matchmaker again. It's not fair." Amy played the daughter card, knowing her mother hated to be accused of being unfair to either of her daughters.

"There's a difference between trying to promote a good relationship with a stranger and meddling in my daughter's love life—or lack thereof." She sniffed indignantly, but it didn't fool Amy.

"Please tell me you didn't invite him to a family dinner," she said with a sinking feeling.

"I did not. All I did was suggest maybe he could have dinner with you and me some evening. He seemed to like the idea."

"You didn't!"

Amy's dread grew as her mother refused to answer. "When are you planning to spring the trap?"

"I'm not planning any such thing. In fact, I've thought of an alternative. Maybe we should discuss this when you're in a more reasonable mood."

"Mom!"

"All I have is a casual suggestion. You can tell him I'm such a lousy cook, you're going to have mercy on him and fix dinner yourself at your apartment."

"That's totally bogus. You're a great cook, and I'd rather mop floors."

"Give it some thought, dear. After all, he took you out to dinner once. You owe him a return invitation."

Amy fumed, but there was no point explaining to her mother that wasn't the way dating worked. For one thing, it had been more than thirty years since her parents had met and fallen in love at first sight—well, after a few good looks anyway. And her father had never planned to skip off to California in two years.

"I'm thinking about it right now, and it's a terrible idea. Please, Mom, give it a rest. I have a full schedule with work and . . . "

And what? The truth was her social life was pretty lame at the moment, the one downside in having a great job in a small town she loved.

"Yes, I know. I'm interfering. Forgive me for wanting a happy future for my daughter." Now her mother's feelings were hurt.

"I love you, Mom. Maybe someday I'll meet Hannah's Prince Charming, but I don't think he'll be Dan Prince."

Her mother chatted about other things for a few minutes, but it was obvious her heart wasn't in the conversation. It was a relief when she hung up.

*

Dan wasn't surprised to get a call from his mother shortly after he got home. She was still at work in California, but someone had told her about the tornado warning in Iowa.

"It looked so dangerous there," she said, not reassured by his voice on the phone.

"I had to take cover in a basement, but so did everyone else in town," he explained. "Anyway, often tornados touch down in the countryside with very little damage. It's only a precaution."

"Ever since you went away to college, I've kept a close watch on the storms out there. I'll be glad when you're back here to stay."

"So will I, Mom. Things are pretty quiet here."

"Do you like the work?" She had a knack for getting to the core of things.

Did he? He started to answer but realized the negative answer he would've given a week ago wasn't the whole truth. So far, his patients had come to him with minor ailments—or imaginary ones if the person was only curious to meet the new doctor. But even without handling a serious crisis, he'd found satisfaction in helping people. And he couldn't deny it was gratifying to be appreciated.

"It's good to be practicing on my own," he said in a guarded voice.

"Are the people nice? Just a second, dear." She interrupted the call to answer a question from someone who came into her office at the museum, giving him a moment to frame his answer.

"Well, are they?" she repeated.

"Yes, very nice." He told her about visiting the day care centers and then switched the topic to news from his brother.

She wasn't easily put off. "Have you met any nice young women?"

"Everyone has been friendly."

It wasn't the answer she was fishing for, and he felt a little guilty for putting her off. She'd only met Belinda once, and they hadn't hit it off at all well, not that his mother tried to run his social life. Without actually saying so, she was hoping to see him settled with a nice wife and a couple of kids.

After their conversation ended, he wondered why he hadn't mentioned his date with Amy. It would've reassured his mother to know he had some semblance of a social life, but he didn't know what to say about her. If he said she was adorable, entertaining, and sexy, it would only be a half-truth. She wasn't his type, and she could be annoying, especially when she overstepped her role as a pharmacist.

Horse liniment! Who'd heard of a drug store dispensing animal remedies?

His stomach was growling after the eventful afternoon, but the contents of his small fridge didn't offer much in the way of dinner. He could go to the market, but that meant cooking for himself. Or he could go to one of the town's lackluster restaurants. Either way, he didn't like eating alone, but he opted for a meal out because it was quicker.

"What I need is a dog," he said, a surprising thought but an option to prevent having all his meals by himself.

Quickly dismissing that idea because he wasn't home enough to care for a pet, he resigned himself to another dinner out. But he just wasn't in the mood to go out by himself.

Face it, he thought, you're getting tired of your own company. Maybe he should think about asking Amy to join him again. There was a void in his life right now, and her image kept popping into his head. Did that mean he was interested in her? Sure it did! But was it a good idea to get emotionally attached when he knew his tenure here would end in two years?

I can't live like a hermit, he told himself, but he knew it was only an excuse. He wanted to see the little pharmacist again. She was playing a big part in his daydreams lately, especially visions of her skinny-dipping at the gravel pit or soaking wet in her little white jacket. What she lacked in height, she more than made up for in curves and cuteness.

On impulse, he picked up his phone where her number was already on speed dial. After nine rings, she hadn't answered. Where could she be in her small apartment? Maybe in the shower, but that brought up images he didn't want to deal with.

"Hello." She answered just when he was about to give up.

He hadn't thought ahead about what to say, but an apology was always a good opener.

"Amy, this is Dan. I'm sorry about this afternoon—being so put out about the horse liniment. I realize it wasn't your idea. Don't give up on me. I'll get the hang of how things are done here eventually."

There was nothing but silence on her end of the line.

"Thanks for letting me share your tornado shelter. We had a few warnings in Iowa City, but there were plenty of big buildings on the university campus."

He obviously wasn't getting anywhere, so he tried one more time.

"I'm going out for some dinner. Can I pick you up to join me?"

"Thanks, but I've eaten. I'm hunkered down reading a book in my bathrobe, so I'd rather not go out this evening."

"I understand." He knew rejection when he heard it. There was nothing to do but end the conversation. "I'll see you around."

"Wait!"

"What?" He was so surprised by the urgency in her voice, he kept listening.

"I owe you a meal," she said.

Did she want to buy dinner for him?

"I'm not much of a cook, but maybe you'd take the risk and have dinner here some evening."

"Sure, sounds great. I'm not a fussy eater." Why had he added that bit? It made it sound as if he expected her meal to be lousy. "When do you want me?"

"Thursday is my day off this week. Would that be okay?"

Was that hesitation he heard in her voice? Just in case she was already regretting her impulsive invitation, he quickly agreed to it.

"I'll see you then," she said, breaking off the call.

For several moments he stood with the phone in hand, wondering what was up with her. Did she feel obligated to offer him a meal? Had she expected him to decline? He couldn't help imagining her snuggled beside him with nothing between them but a fluffy robe. Was the temperature rising, or had it been too long for him?

He jammed the cell phone into the pocket of his jeans and headed toward the market, hoping they had one of their special roasted chickens left. He was in no fit mood to sit around a restaurant.

*

What on earth had she done? Amy hadn't intended to ask Dan to her apartment for dinner. The invitation just popped out, an impulse she was already regretting. He'd caught her at a weak moment, almost asleep on the couch with a book unread on her lap.

Not only did she have to come up with something to feed him, she had to tell her mother. She could already hear her mother's glee, and it would be impossible to explain why she'd done it when she didn't even know herself.

Shivering at the thought of being alone with Dan in her digs, she let her imagination run amuck. Suddenly everything in her apartment shrunk in size when she compared it to his commanding masculine presence, his long legs, broad muscular chest, and devastating smile. There was so much of him to admire, and the more she thought of the parts she hadn't seen, the more uncomfortable she became. She'd feel the same way if a hunky hero stepped down from a movie screen to whisk her into the bedroom. The prospect was as daunting as it was unreal.

Tomorrow was soon enough to let her mother know. Or maybe the day after would suffice. This was one episode in her life that she absolutely did not want to become fodder for the town's gossips!

CHAPTER 9

Why on earth had she asked Dan to come Thursday? Every hour that passed increased her nervousness, and it would've been so much better to get it over with right away. What could it possibly matter whether she had the day off when he came to dinner?

As it was, she avoided him like the plague in the days leading up to their "date," checking the street before venturing outside, hiding in the stock room when he came into the store, and generally acting like an idiot. It was embarrassing beyond belief to realize he probably thought she was coming on to him. Nothing good could come of this. It would be a disaster, and she'd have to spend the next two years avoiding him.

Dan was out of her league and destined to reject her sooner or later. When he was free to go back to California, he probably wouldn't remember her name. She was setting herself up for heartbreak.

Or maybe she was overreacting. A guy with his great looks was probably used to female pursuit. Maybe her invitation was so inconsequential he'd forget to come.

Yes, that would be perfect. If he stood her up, she'd never have to deal with him again. Her feelings would be hurt, especially since she'd been cleaning her apartment every evening to be ready for him, but wasn't that immensely better than suffering a broken heart when he left town for good?

"My mother is having a Pots and Pans party this evening," Josie said Thursday afternoon. "I guess I have to go. Want to keep me company? You don't have to buy anything."

"Thanks, but I'll pass. Kitchen stuff really isn't my thing." Amy avoided looking directly at her friend. Josie knew her well enough to suspect she was up to something.

"Mine either, at least not that high-priced stuff. I told Mom it's too expensive, but she's excited about getting a free pasta pot for hosting the party."

"Well, have fun." Amy hoped she sounded chipper.

By ten minutes after six she'd done all her closing jobs, including checking the registers early and putting the proceeds in a bank bag to drop off in the night depository on the way home.

This still didn't leave her much time to get ready, but she had it all planned. All she had to do was get herself ready.

When she was still damp from the shower with her hair hanging in unruly curls from the moisture, she faced her closet with determination. Fancy was out. Much as she'd like to wow Dan with her form-fitting black dress or the sleeveless pink cotton knit that barely covered her behind, she had to be sensible. Casual dress would send a better message.

After a few moments of agonizing, she opted for her best white shorts and a bright pink tank top. After dressing and slipping into sandals, she rushed to set the kitchen table. Her plastic plates and stainless tableware weren't elegant, but neither was the menu.

"There, I'm ready," she announced aloud.

There was even time for a light makeup job to make her eyes look more dramatic and her lips more kissable—not that there would be any of that. She crossed her fingers for the first time since grade school and hoped the evening wouldn't be a total disaster.

*

Dan kept reminding himself Amy wasn't his type. Sure, she was cute, cuddly, and quick-witted, the perfect date for a senior prom, but he wasn't a horny teenager. He liked sleek brunettes with wicked eyes, mysterious beauties who left much to be discovered. Belinda had been his ideal until he discovered her treachery and greed. She wanted to marry a filthy rich big-city doctor, but she hadn't been willing to stay with him while he fulfilled his obligation to Heart City and established himself in California.

Thinking about Belinda put him in a decidedly foul state of mind. He even considered canceling dinner at Amy's because he didn't want to inflict his grouchy mood on her. But how could he back out at the last minute after she went to the trouble of fixing a meal for him?

A shower made him feel cleaner but not much happier about dinner. In his experience, an invitation for a home-cooked meal had awkward connotations. He hardly knew the pharmacist, and the scenario was a little too cozy for comfort. Next she'd be inviting him to her mother's house to meet the family.

His wardrobe was nothing to write home about, although Belinda had often given him gifts she "picked up" at Macy's in Chicago when she went into the city from her ritzy suburban home. He'd begged her not to, but apparently, his wardrobe didn't meet her standards. That should have been his first clue.

After deciding on khaki slacks and a navy polo shirt, he went to his van, feeling a bit silly for driving the short distance. But he felt less conspicuous in a vehicle, and one thing he'd already learned about Heart City: The town had eyes. He didn't want Amy to be embarrassed by casual gossip, and his van was nondescript enough not to attract attention.

When he got to her apartment and tapped softly on her door, he was surprised to be kept waiting. He knocked again more forcefully, wondering if she was playing the old female game of make-him-wait.

"Sorry," she said, sounding breathless when she opened the door. "I was in the middle of something."

"No problem. I thought you might like to try some California wine." It had been a last minute thought. A friend had given him a bottle to celebrate the beginning of his practice, and he forgotten about it until he was ready to leave for Amy's.

"Thank you," she said with a broad smile. "I never thought of getting some. I'm afraid I don't have a corkscrew. The only wine I ever buy has a cap."

"That's okay. Save it for another day."

He looked around her compact but pleasant living area. It was sparsely furnished with several Renoir prints framed over a green and gold striped couch. There were two rockers, one antique and the other with clean lines in keeping with the couch. The floor had wide aged oak boards, perhaps original to the building, and she'd had the good taste to use it as part of the décor instead of covering it with rugs.

"Nice place," he said, liking the lack of clutter and the sunny vista through the open sliding glass door to the small balcony.

"Thanks, I enjoy it. I only have to pop the potatoes in the microwave," she said, not allowing any time for chitchat before the meal. "If you'd like to wait on the balcony, I put a chair out there."

"I'm fine here."

He stood, hands stuffed in his pants pockets, watching as she bent over to check the contents of the oven. Her legs and butt were spectacular, and the shorts hugged her cheeks in a more provocative way than she seemed to realize.

"Won't be long now." She straightened and smiled a bit self-consciously. "Don't expect too much. I'll never be on the Food Network."

"I'm surprised. All that lab work you had to do for your pharmacy degree."

"Chemistry is not cooking," she said with a grin, the first sign she might enjoy the evening.

He gave her high marks for efficiency. Less than ten minutes after he arrived, she had dinner on the table. Or maybe she regretted her invitation and wanted to get it over with.

His jaw fell open, and he nearly laughed out loud when he saw the golden brown chicken, slow-cooked on a spit at the neighborhood market.

"I'm not much at carving," she said apologetically as she plunked the poultry on a plate. "Want to give it a try?"

"Sure."

Her big carving knife and sharp-pronged fork seemed like overkill for such a small bird, but he gave it a go. In fact, he'd consumed an identical chicken over the last three days.

"How did you get all the way to Iowa for school?" she asked as she struggled to remove the plastic from a potato without burning her fingers.

"Long story, but not an interesting one. Basically, I followed the scholarship money. My mother's boss at the museum got his undergraduate degree at the University of Iowa. He helped a lot." He passed the plate of dismembered chicken across the table to her.

"That's nice." She passed him a bowl of salad, the kind that came in a bag, and watched him use two soup spoons to put some on a separate plate.

"You've always lived in Heart City?" he asked.

"Except for college."

The conversation was going nowhere. Polite was overrated when it came to getting to know a woman.

"Why aren't you married?" It was a question calculated to rile her and end this stilted exchange.

"I beg your pardon?" The green glints in her eyes sparkled as she reacted indignantly.

"It's a fair question," he said, taking a bite of chicken so dry he had to wash it down with ice water. What had she done to make a fairly decent roasted bird so tough?

"No one has asked me," she said in a dismissive voice.

"I doubt that." He tried the potato and decided it really needed a big dollop of sour cream to make it edible.

"No one I wanted to marry," she said. "There are lots of advantages to being single."

"Like what?" He was baiting her, but it covered his indifference to the meal.

"I'm not accountable to anyone, except my boss, of course." She nibbled on a bite of chicken and seemed to have the same reaction he did. "This is terrible. I thought I could rely on the ones the market does on a spit."

"It is a little dry," he said, enjoying the banter far more than the dinner. "More so than the one I ate the last three days."

"Really?" Her cheeks flushed with embarrassment, making her look even more delectable.

"I shouldn't have mentioned it. Sorry." He did feel a little bad.

"At least I won't have to sit here and pretend to eat it," she said with a grin. "Guess I set the oven too high. I wanted to be sure it was hot, so 500 degrees seemed about right."

"The salad looks good." She'd set out grated cheese, croutons, and three different kinds of bottled dressing.

"I hope something is. Why aren't you married? You probably had a string of women dying to marry a doctor." She was playing hardball, and he admired it, even if her question touched a sensitive nerve.

"Just one. She had visions of a big income and a ritzy lifestyle, but no patience to wait for it."

"She wouldn't come to Heart City with you?"

"Wouldn't even consider it."

"I'm sorry. You must hate being here without her," she said sympathetically.

"No," he said, giving some thought to her comment. "I can see I'm needed here. There's a lot to be said for that."

"Maybe she'll miss you and change her mind," Amy suggested, sounding genuinely concerned for him.

"Too late for that." He stood, his appetite gone. "How about ordering a pizza delivery? We can have salad while we wait."

"It isn't the dinner I planned, but it sounds good. If I ever do get married, he'd better be a good cook."

"Men don't marry women for their culinary skills," he said in a teasing voice. "Who makes the best pizza in town?"

"Joe's Stop and Go. I have the number on my fridge."

"The gas station?" Small-town Iowa was full of surprises.

"He started out with gas pumps and a small convenience store, but his pizza slices were so popular he added a big kitchen at the rear and began delivery. Now his brother runs the rest of the business, and all Joe does is make pizza."

"Interesting." Actually it was. It never would've occurred to him to order pizza where he bought gas.

He took his ever-present phone out of his pants pocket, hoping he wouldn't get any emergency calls this evening. He was beginning to see the potential for enjoying himself with Amy, and now that he wasn't faced with a dehydrated chicken, he felt hungry.

"What do you like?" he asked.

"White pizza with shrimp and scallops." She didn't hesitate. He liked a woman who knew what she wanted.

"They have that at Joe's?"

"Hey, we may be small-town people, but that doesn't mean our palates are numb. I doubt you can name a topping Joe can't provide."

"How about Mexican?"

"As hot as you can stand."

"Five cheese."

"Name them."

"Vegan?"

"He might surprise you there, especially when zucchini is in season."

"Okay, I concede. I like plain old sausage, green peppers, mushrooms, and onions, plus a good aged cheese. And thick crust. But I wouldn't mind a piece of yours too."

"I'm good about sharing." She grinned at him and started to clear the table, leaving the salad fixings out.

"Why are you bagging the chicken?" he asked.

"For my neighbor's cat. That beastie is a carnivore if I've ever seen one."

"You don't like cats?" He preferred dogs himself, but Belinda had kept some nasty-tempered felines.

"I like them fine, but Mom is allergic to them. We never had a cat, but I grew up with a Boston terrier. I cried buckets when he passed away."

"I seem to recall you cry at weddings too." He grinned because he was having more fun than he'd anticipated.

"You saw that?" She covered her face with her hands and peeked out between her fingers, a childlike but absolutely charming gesture.

"When you're a stranger at a reception, you notice a lot of things. Your niece, for instance, is a doll. I wouldn't mind half a dozen like her someday." He exaggerated, but kids had always figured in his plans for the future.

"Six daughters! I never would've guessed you want to start your own basketball team."

"Well, maybe not six, and I don't care whether I have girls or boys. But I love kids. They're so honest and fresh, so ready to learn about the world. My nephews are my favorite people in the world."

"That's nice. I adore Hannah—even if she is a born matchmaker at age seven."

"She wants you to get married?"

"Oh, no, it's worse than that. She wants me to marry Prince Charming and ride off into the sunset on his snow-white steed the way it happens in her fairy tale books."

"I'd like to have a talk with that girl," Dan said laughing. "My nephews still think girls are lower order creatures, somewhere below tree toads and grasshoppers."

"No doubt they'll change their minds eventually." Amy's light laughter made him tingle.

When the pizza came twenty minutes later, he had to give her credit for knowing where to get the best. He wolfed down four large pieces, each one tasting better than the last. She was right about the white pizza too. It was better than what he'd had in urban areas.

Afterward they made a pretense of watching TV, but he scarcely noticed what was flickering across the screen. They talked about music, movies, books, and their experiences as university students.

"You keep surprising me," he said after the sun went down and they were still sitting side-by-side on her couch in the dim light.

"You never expected me to be such a horrible cook?" Her grin told him she was beyond hurt feelings.

Her full pink lips were just too tempting. He stood and pulled her up with him, leaning down to slowly kiss her.

"Oh my." She looked stunned.

He cupped her chin, loving the softness of her skin and the faint scent of a flowery perfume. When her lips parted under his, he felt a dazzling moment of pleasure before reality intruded.

This had gone too far. Amy was too cute, too sweet, and too trusting. They couldn't have a casual affair. He instinctively knew he'd end up hurting her if he let things get out of control.

"I have to go." He stepped away and retrieved the phone he'd left on her kitchen counter.

After thanking her for the dinner invitation, he left abruptly. It wasn't the way he wanted the evening to end: It was the way it had to end.

CHAPTER 10

"How was your date last night?" Josie gave her a sly grin as they got ready to open the store for the day on Friday.

"What date?" The last thing Amy wanted to talk about was her dinner with Dan. After all, what was there to say? They'd kissed, and he raced out of her apartment like a man who'd just sat on a hot burner.

"Come on," her friend urged, "I know he had dinner at your place. My cousin Doug delivers pizza for Joe's."

"I take it discretion isn't one of the job requirements." Amy felt put out by Josie's curiosity, her cousin's big mouth, and the way she felt about Dan.

Why kiss her and run away? Did she disappoint him? Or was he afraid she'd expect something from him just because they'd shared a single brief moment?

Life would be so much simpler if she lived in a big city. A person could have a fling, and no one would notice or care.

"Did you have a good time?" Josie asked, never one to let a subject drop before she was satisfied.

"The pizza was great, as always. You'd better start the coffee. We open in a few minutes." Amy played the boss card, unwilling to share any part of the evening with her friend or anyone else.

"I have big news," Josie said. "Gayle Briggs is pregnant. They've been trying forever, so she didn't tell anyone until now. She's five months along and only beginning to show."

"That's so nice for her," Amy said, glad for their former teammate on the cheerleading squad and even happier to drop the subject of Dan.

"She's been seeing a fertility specialist in Des Moines," Josie said, starting to ready the soda fountain for the morning coffee drinkers. "Since she's had so much trouble, she's going to have the baby there. She'll stay at an aunt's house when her time gets close."

"I'll call and congratulate her after work," Amy said. "She and Greg will make great parents."

"Brad and I have been talking about starting a family too," Josie said. "I told him my clock is ticking, but he wants to save up more money first."

"You're still young," Amy said. "I have to get to work now."

Retreating to the pharmacy department in the rear of the store, she couldn't keep her mind on the morning routine. Josie's baby talk had reminded her of Dan's comment about children. Some woman would be very fortunate to have him as the father of her babies, but she would probably be some beautiful, sophisticated Californian.

Her first customer was Gracie Fields, the president of the PTA for an eon or so. Although her children were grown up and living in other places, Gracie didn't relinquish the gavel at the elementary school all four of them had attended. Given that no one else wanted the job, she was a shoo-in year after year.

"Good morning, Amy." The round-faced, curly-headed woman looked anything but presidential in her orange sundress and green flip-flops. "Dr. Prince called in a prescription for me yesterday, but I couldn't get here to pick it up."

"No problem," Amy said, finding it in the bin. "I have it ready for you. Did the doctor tell you to be sure to drink lots of water while you're taking it?"

"Oh, yes, he gave me very specific instructions," the customer said. "Did you enjoy your date with the doctor?"

How did a casual acquaintance like Gracie Fields know about something that happened the night before? Did someone put it on Facebook, or were the phone lines buzzing this early in the day?

"We had pizza is all," Amy said, probably telling the woman something she already knew. "It wasn't a date."

"He stayed quite a while," Gracie said, pretending to read the printed instructions that came with her pills.

Shoulders slumping in resignation, Amy could only shake her head.

"The secretary of the PTA happened to be visiting her aunt in your building," Gracie said matter-of-factly. Apparently it never occurred to her that she was a nosy busybody, Amy thought.

"That will be forty-two dollars," Amy said.

"My, I'm sure it wasn't that much last time I had this infection. Of course, that must have been around 1998, the year my great uncle Herman passed on."

Amy tried to tune out the stream of idle chitchat, but she was too annoyed by the gossiping woman to concentrate. Did everyone in town know about the dinner with Dan?

She accepted Heart City as a place where everyone knew everyone else's business. Once it had felt comforting to be part of a close-knit community, and people usually backed up their curiosity with genuine concern for the welfare of others. Now it felt stifling to have her every move be public business. But she had to remember, this was the "white-picket fence" kind of life she'd always wanted. The buzz about Dan would soon go away. He was only passing through on the way to his real life.

The rest of the morning dragged, and her thoughts kept coming back to Dan. His kisses had disturbed her, no question about that. She'd been disappointed by his abrupt departure, although it was understandable. Heart City wasn't the kind of place where people had casual affairs under the radar, especially not a doctor who was very much in the public eye.

When she had a few idle moments, she let her imagination run wild. What if they did live in a big city? They could have a passionate fling, and no one would know or care. She wouldn't have to spend the rest of her life wondering how it would be to make love with Dan.

When was a customer not a customer? Amy watched her mother make her way through the store directly toward the pharmacy counter. Alice Crane was not there to shop.

"Am I the last one in town to know about your date?" Her

mother sounded hurt and her blue eyes were moist as she confronted her daughter.

"I'm sorry, Mom. It wasn't a big deal. I just took your advice and invited him over for dinner. Unfortunately my meal was terrible, and we ordered out for pizza."

"I would've been happy to help you out. You know how tired I am of cooking for one. I could've made pasta and meatballs and shared with you." Her mother ran her hand over her windblown hair, a lighter blonde than Amy's because she regularly used the packaged hair coloring for sale in the drug store.

"Mom, it was just a casual, spur-of-the-moment thing." Amy felt a little guilty about varnishing the truth, but she didn't want her mother to feel bad.

"Well, I'm happy you're starting to have some social life here," her mother said. "I worry you're eventually going to be bored and look for a job someplace more exciting."

"You know I love my job," Amy assured her. "And I love living close to you and the rest of the family. I'd hate to miss watching Hannah grow up."

"You can't let us hold you back if opportunity presents itself," her mother assured her. She wasn't talking about the job market. "Did the two of you have a nice time?"

"We had Joe's delicious pizza and a nice conversation. He went home early." She had to give her mother something to think about, however sketchy the account was.

One thing about gossip: It was here today and gone tomorrow. Since she and Dan were unlikely to spend more time together, the rumors would fade away, and life could get back to normal. She hoped.

*

Every morning when he woke up, Dan regretted leaving Amy so abruptly on the night of their date. His evenings home alone seemed especially lonely when he thought about her.

A week passed, and somehow he hadn't gotten so much as a glimpse of her. Was she avoiding him? He wouldn't blame her. He couldn't even pretend to himself their kisses had only been a friendly gesture.

Although he'd never met a woman like her, he knew instinctively she couldn't handle casual sex. He wanted to sneak away with her to a motel in a neighboring town as though they were naughty teenagers, but that was a bad idea. She would read too much into it, and he didn't want to hurt her when he left. The two years would fly by if he gave in to his intense feelings for her, but the bottom line was that she belonged in Heart City, Iowa, and he didn't.

Friday office hours had been especially busy that week, mainly because kids were heading off to summer camps and needed physical forms filled out. He loved that part of his practice and spent more time with each child than was strictly necessary. It was a way to make friends with young patients before they were sick or injured.

Besides the usual junk, his mail slot in the main foyer of the converted Victorian house had a couple of personal pieces. One he ripped open as soon as he got inside his apartment. His nephews had both drawn pictures of Uncle Dan the doctor, and he had a good laugh at their comic caricatures.

The smaller envelope was a bit puzzling. He'd never heard of Gayle and Greg Briggs, and he'd certainly never been to a couples' baby shower. A little note at the bottom explained why he'd gotten the invitation:

"Please escort Amy Crane."

"What the . . . !" he said aloud. When had they become a couple, and why would complete strangers invite him to a baby shower?

After ordering a pizza, he mulled over the odd summons. Would Amy be the only woman without a date if he didn't go? Certainly he didn't want to be there, but were they good friends of hers? Had she suggested him as an escort because she wanted to see him again? The idea didn't bother him as much as he would've thought. In fact, he'd been looking for an excuse to see her again, if only to make things right between them.

His pizza came; he was trying the white sauce with shrimp and scallops and extra mushrooms. It had great flavor, but somehow he didn't enjoy it as much as he had the piece he'd tried at Amy's apartment. After the leftovers were in the fridge, he made up his mind to sound her out on the invitation.

"Hello." Her voice was melodic on the phone, and he could imagine her holding it to her ear, soft blonde curls spilling over her cheek.

"Hi, this is Dan Prince."

"Actually, you're the only Dan I know," she said in an expressionless voice.

Was she angry or disinterested? He rarely got that kind of reception when he called a woman, but he probably deserved it. He hadn't been exactly tactful about running out after some really hot kisses.

"I have a little puzzle here," he said.

"I got the shower invitation too. You don't have to go. They shouldn't have assumed we were a couple." Was she letting him off the hook, or did she genuinely not want to go with him?

"I've never been to a couples' baby shower—never heard of it to be honest. I guess it could be fun."

"Are you saying you want to go?" She sounded surprised.

"Well, yeah, I guess so. I mean, it's something different to do. The mother-to-be isn't a patient of mine, so there's no reason not to."

"You don't have to. I'm sure I can get someone else or go alone. The men will just stand around talking to each other anyway, if it's like the usual mixed event here."

"Look," he said, "I'd like to go with you. If that bothers you, I'll forget it."

"I suppose it would make Gayle happy. She's gone through a lot to get pregnant—even went to a fertility specialist in Des Moines."

"Wednesday evening, right? Can I pick you up? I don't know where this address is." They weren't getting anywhere debating it, he decided.

"It's tricky to find. They rent a small place behind a big farm house, so if you don't know what to look for, you can drive right past it," she said.

"Then I'll rely on you to get me there. What about a gift? Should we go in together? I'm clueless about baby clothes and stuff."

"I'll put together a package of necessities from the drug store, diapers, powder, wipes, things like that. It can be from both of us. They'll probably get enough tiny baby garments to clothe quintuplets."

"That's settled then," he said, surprised by how much he looked forward to seeing Amy again.

"Okay."

"You wouldn't like to have dinner with me tomorrow, would you?" he asked without giving it any thought.

"No, thank you." Her business-like tone told him exactly where he stood with her. "We'll need twenty minutes to get to the shower. I can drive if you like."

"No thanks." He remembered her high-speed driving on the day of the tornado warning. "I'll pick you up."

"I'll be outside waiting," she said, saying a quick good-bye.

What message was she sending? He wasn't used to picking up women on the street, but then, she probably didn't see this as a date. If her description of "mixed events" in Heart City was right, it was middle school all over, the boys in one room and the girls in the other.

"Well, Prince, you've got yourself a non-date to go to some small-town coed baby shower," he said to himself.

He didn't know why he felt so happy about it.

CHAPTER 11

The first thing Dan heard when he and Amy pulled up beside a green pickup on the farm property was a metallic clink followed by male jeers.

"Feel free to join the men," Amy said, speaking for the first time in the last ten minutes. "I guess horseshoes are the grown-up boys' version of pin the tail on the donkey."

"I don't have to be here," he said, giving vent to his growing irritation. She acted as though he'd forced himself on her when he'd only come as a courtesy.

"Just remember, this wasn't my idea," she said as she got out of his van and started walking toward the noisy group. She rejected his offer to carry a large box wrapped in blue paper with baby angels—or maybe they were cupids. He'd never bothered to distinguish between them.

"You didn't try to talk me out of it," he pointed out, taking long strides to catch up.

"I told you there wouldn't be much mingling of the sexes, so go circulate. I'll join the women. Apparently the landlords have loaned their parlor because Gayle and Greg don't have room for a big group." She stalked off toward a bunch of balloons on the porch of the large two-story yellow farmhouse.

Everywhere he looked, fields were green with corn, the stalks already knee-high or taller. In spite of his big-city upbringing, he marveled at the unbroken vista of growing plants. He'd heard that each stalk of field corn only produced one ear, but huge silos would fill with golden kernels at the end of the season. He looked forward to harvest time when big wagons would haul the corn to Heart City to be dried and eventually sold. He'd been there long enough to know the railroad cars full of corn were the lifeblood of the town.

Dan had never been shy, but he still felt uncomfortable approaching a group of men who were mostly strangers. He didn't feel part of the community, and these friends who all knew each other made him feel more of an outsider.

"Hey, Doc!" The recent groom, Judson Carter, stopped hooting at the failure of a burly redhead to wrap a horseshoe around a stake in the ground and called out to him.

"Judson, nice to see you," Dan said, appreciating the welcome. He almost asked how the honeymoon was but decided he didn't know the man well enough. Who knew what constituted prying in rural Iowa?

"You can be on my team," Judson said. "We're a man short."

"I'll give it a try," he said, although he'd never played it. How hard could it be to toss a horseshoe?

He watched the technique—or lack thereof—of a few players before it was his turn. Meanwhile, Judson introduced him to a few of the others, including the father-to-be. The majority were young farmers but there was also a construction worker, a plumber, and a guy who ran the garden center with his father. Ordinarily, he'd only meet them as patients, but being part of this group made him feel younger and more relaxed.

His first throw was way off, but with encouragement from his team, he finally landed a horseshoe around the stake.

"Way to go, Doc," Judson said.

"Call me Dan." He felt surprisingly proud of himself for scoring.

When a portly middle-aged woman came out on the porch and called out for the men to come inside, Dan would've preferred to stay outside pitching horseshoes. A grumble or two told him he wasn't alone there.

How was he supposed to act with Amy? Should he pretend they really were a couple? Or maybe they could ignore each other without attracting attention. After all, they weren't the guests of honor.

The sun was hot, and he could feel his white polo shirt clinging to his back. Why did the women want this sweaty group of men to join them? He clenched his jaw and prepared to endure whatever came next.

*

Amy dug her nails into her palms, not sure what to expect from Dan when the men came inside. Much to her relief, the women's conversation had been all about babies and Gayle's struggle to get pregnant. Every mother there had to relate her birth experiences, and Amy found herself pretty much left out of the talk that swirled around her.

Would that change when Dan came inside? She desperately hoped they wouldn't have to play any silly boy-girl games that would stir up people's curiosity about their relationship—or lack thereof.

"Hi." He came to stand beside her as the men mingled with their spouses and girlfriends.

"Enjoy the horseshoes?" she asked for lack of anything else to say.

Unlike most of the men, he hadn't worn a hat outside. His face was flushed and his dark hair was moist and clung to his forehead in curly tendrils. When the hostess, Mrs. Lacey, offered him a glass of hand-squeezed lemonade from a tray, he took it gratefully and downed half of it in one big gulp.

She'd never seen him sweaty and red-faced. Much to her surprise, it only made him hotter in the I-want-to-jump-your-bones way. This was not good. Instead of blending in, he stood out like a Greek god, and she wasn't the only woman who noticed.

"I'm Gayle Briggs," her pregnant friend said to Dan. "I'm so happy you could join us. Because of all my problems, I'm giving birth in Des Moines, but I do hope you'll provide care for the baby when he arrives."

"I'd be pleased to," Dan said, apparently oblivious of the attention he was attracting from the female guests.

Not that she was jealous, Amy told herself. She was done with Dr. Prince, and he'd better know she had nothing to do with roping him into this party.

"Okay, boys and girls," Marge, Gayle's mother, said. "We have one game all of you can play, then our mom and dad-to-be will open their gifts."

Her heart sinking, Amy hoped it wasn't some silly charade that would call more attention to Dan or her.

"Doreen made this up herself," Marge said, nodding at one of the single women. "Here's how it goes. Everyone make a big circle."

Even in the roomy parlor, it was a bit of a squeeze. Amy managed to take a position several spots away from Dan. If this involved teaming up, she would pick Logan from the feed store or one of the other single men, safer choices than the doctor.

"Here's how it works," Doreen said, preening when she became the center of attention. "Pretend this is a hot potato."

She held up a beanbag in the shape of a cat and wiggled in her ultra-short crimson dress. Doreen was the town's self-styled vamp, and any game she invented was likely to have suggestive undertones.

"You can toss it at anyone in the room. Mrs. Lacey is going to play music while this is going on." She nodded at the landlady sitting at the upright piano in one corner of the room. "When the music stops, whoever has the bean bag can kiss the person of his or her choice. Then those two are eliminated, and the game goes on. There's a prize for the last couple standing."

Doreen made a big deal of counting to be sure there were an equal number of men and women. A few of the older guests had wisely opted not to play.

Music boomed, the bean bag flew around the circle, and Amy wanted to go home. When the bag landed against her chest, she passed it on as if it were burning hot but not to Dan. That's what her face would be if she had to kiss him in front of all these people.

The first person to catch it was a man who dared his wife's wrath to kiss the guest of honor, Gayle. People hooted and cheered, even though his kiss was so chaste not even his spouse could object.

Mandy, wearing her glasses on the tip of her nose, was the next to get caught with the bean bag. She planted a noisy, enthusiastic kiss on her new husband's lips. It went over well with the other guests.

The circle grew smaller, and Amy grew more nervous. She'd rather kiss any other man in the room than go through the embarrassment of being Dan's choice. Her best hope was that he'd choose someone else, given that their ride there hadn't been exactly cordial.

When Doreen got to choose, Amy hoped Dan would be her choice. It was her big chance to make a play for the doctor, and her "date" was really her second cousin, probably doing her a favor by coming with her.

Instead, the town's biggest flirt planted a noisy kiss on the father-to-be. Greg didn't seem to mind, at least not until he caught his wife's eye.

The eliminated guests were having a great time, calling out encouragement and cheering when the kisses were especially emphatic. The circle had closed now with only six players left. Dan had a firm grip of Amy's hand, or she might have tried to duck out of the game. When the bean bag came to her, she threw it frantically, and then realized she should try to keep it. She could give one of the other two men a peck on the cheek and be done with it.

The music, simple numbers Amy hadn't heard since elementary school, came to an abrupt stop, and Dan dangled the bean bag from his fingers.

"Your turn, Dan," Judson called out with glee.

Amy wanted to put her fist in his mouth. Her only hope was that Dan would choose Josie because she was cute or Gayle's cousin from Dubuque who might have hurt feelings if she was the last one kissed. From what she knew of him, Dan was a kind person.

Before she could second-guess his choice, he spun her around into his arms and brought his lips down hard on hers. She opened her mouth to protest. Wrong move. His tongue slid deeply into her mouth while his lips did wonderful things to hers. She almost lost herself in his demanding kiss, but laughter and shouts of encouragement brought her back to the cold reality of the game.

"That is enough!" She pushed hard on his chest until he released her.

If he'd intended to embarrass her, he'd succeeded. She wanted to sink into a deep hole where she couldn't hear the congratulatory comments or the appreciative whistles. Before she could run from the room, Dan took her hand in his and pulled her to the back of the group. The last four people still had to compete for the prize. When it turned out to be a coupon for six free car washes, the crowd's attention turned to talk about what a good prize it was.

"Now it's time for the mommy and daddy to open their gifts," Mrs. Lacey said. The landlady and her quiet husband had five grandchildren, but it didn't diminish her enthusiasm for babies—anyone's babies.

When all the parlor furniture and a number of folding chairs where occupied, the guests still standing sat on the floor, not a hardship because it was covered with thick forest green carpeting to go with an assortment of antique furnishings and a few comfortable modern pieces.

Pulling hard on her short pink skirt to preserve modesty, Amy sat down next to Dan, leaving a comfortable space between them. Trying to avoid him would only make her more conspicuous, but she pointedly ignored him through the lengthy process of opening presents. Maybe because Gayle had waited so long to get pregnant, she seemed determined to take as much time as possible to open each and every package. She peeled off tape, carefully removed ribbons so a friend could save them for her, and opened gift wrap as though it were gold leaf. That was the faster part. She and Greg both exclaimed over every gift, pointing out all the reasons why it was wonderful for their baby.

Dan squirmed, but Amy still ignored him.

"Did you sign my name?" he whispered when they finally came to her gift.

"Yes."

"Then I owe you money."

"Forget it," she hissed.

"Look at all the things we'll really need," Gayle said, pulling each and every item out of the box. "Diapers, baby powder, baby oil, and oh look, ointment for diaper rash. Thank you so much, Amy and Dan."

Well, no one could doubt they were a couple now, Amy thought, wondering how much longer this torture would go on. Dan reached over and patted her knee, which she'd failed to keep covered by the skimpy skirt. She wanted to slap his hand away, but it would only stir up more speculation about their relationship.

After the gift opening ordeal, Amy headed for the restroom, only to find a line of women waiting to use the facility. At least the delay gave her an excuse to avoid Dan for a few minutes.

When she returned to the party, the dining room table was loaded to capacity with good things to eat. Dan was among the first to fill a sturdy throw-away plastic platter, which thrifty Iowa homemakers almost always washed and reused.

"I didn't wait for you," he said, seeking her out even though she tried to be inconspicuous. "Try this."

He lifted a fork to her lips, and she had little choice but to take the morsel of chicken salad with walnuts and grapes. It was one of her favorites, but she could hardly swallow. Feeding her seemed even more intimate than the kiss. Her friends would be expecting wedding invitations before the summer was over, little that they knew.

"Mad at me?" he asked when she turned her head away to refuse any other samples from his plate.

She let her expression answer, narrowing her eyes and pressing her lips into a tight line.

"I'll take that as a yes," he said, not sounding nearly as disturbed as she felt.

A few of the older people left, the first signal the shower was winding down.

"We can leave now," she told Dan, who'd finally had his fill of buffet food.

"A couple of guys are going to throw some more horseshoes," he said. "I won't be long."

Predictably, the separation of the genders left the women inside exclaiming over the gifts and trading pregnancy stories. Amy tried to muster some enthusiasm, but she kept in the background, knowing sooner or later her friends would ask questions about Dan.

It was another hour before Dan came inside to ask if she was ready to go. The leave-taking took another ten minutes as she thanked Gayle's landlady and mother and complimented a few others on the delicious dishes they'd contributed to the buffet. Apparently, her own reputation as a non-cook had excused her from bringing something. Finally, she hugged Gayle and sincerely wished her good luck. In spite of the celebrating, she could tell her friend was nervous about her big venture into motherhood.

Getting into Dan's van before he could open the door for her, she stared straight ahead and didn't say anything. The couples' shower had been a fiasco, but she didn't want to rehash it.

"Well, that was more fun than I expected," he said as he buckled in. "I guess a shower is as good an excuse as any for a party."

"I don't know what you were thinking," she said.

"I tried to get into the spirit of things," he said.

"By—you know."

"By kissing you like I enjoyed it?"

"We're not a couple, and we're not going to be a couple. I don't know why you made such a production of kissing me."

"Because you taste so good?"

"That's no excuse! My friends are going to want a follow-up report, and I have better things to do than trying to convince them we're only acquaintances." She didn't like the way she sounded, but he'd really rattled her.

"Is that what we are?" Either he was a great actor, or he was genuinely puzzled.

"Look, I'm happy with my life here. I had a serious boyfriend once, but it didn't work out. I'd rather things stay the way they are for now. Maybe someday . . . "

"Someday you'll let yourself fall in love?" He was driving so slow it didn't seem as if he wanted to get back to town.

"You'll be long gone by then," she said in a soft voice.

"I met a lot of nice guys today, but I don't see you hooking up with any of them," he said thoughtfully.

"I don't see why not." Really, this conversation was going nowhere.

"You're smart, you're beautiful, and you're ambitious. Someday you'll wake up and realize you're also lonely." He slowed the van to a crawl and pulled off on the side of the road.

"Why are you stopping?" She wanted this conversation to end.

"Because I want you to stop being afraid of me." He turned off the motor and stared at her.

"That's ridiculous! Why would I be afraid of you?" She clenched and unclenched her hands, keeping her eyes averted.

"Because we might get involved, and it might not work out. You're afraid to take a chance." He sounded angry.

"You'll be leaving . . . "

"It has nothing to do with that." He reached over to take her hand, but she pulled it away.

"You had someone, and apparently she dumped you. I don't want to be your consolation prize." There, she'd said it and didn't regret it.

"You must think I'm pretty shallow."

"No, I think you're a good person and probably a competent doctor. That doesn't mean we should have an affair." She wanted to take back the last word, but it was too late.

"Have I asked you to sleep with me?" The intensity in his voice did scare her just a little.

"No."

"I know perfectly well we couldn't keep it a secret in this town, and apparently you care more about gossip than me." He gripped the steering wheel but made no move to restart his vehicle.

"I don't base my life on what people might say," she snapped.

"You could've fooled me. Why else would you be so upset because I kissed you?"

"You practically sucked out my tonsils in front of dozens of people!"

"And you hated it?"

"Yes!"

"I don't believe you," he said, leaning over and taking her head between his palms.

"Stop . . ."

His hands were warm on her cheeks, but not as hot as his lips when he slowly brushed them against hers. She felt helpless in his grip as he teased her lips apart and gently flicked his tongue against hers.

"Is this so awful?" he murmured.

"Noooo." Her heart spoke for her.

"It's time for you to grow up, Amy." He abruptly stopped and pulled away from her.

"That's a terrible thing to say!" She wanted to throttle him or something. If this was his idea of teasing, she hated it.

"Maybe, but you've living in a cocoon, pretending you want life to go on without changing. You see me as a threat because I come from a different world."

"Funny, I didn't know you were a psychiatrist."

"You're not that hard to read, Amy. If I didn't like you so much . . ."

"If this is how you treat someone you like, I'd hate to be on your bad list. Now can we please go?"

"Fine." The starter made a grinding noise before it turned over.

Dan was silent on the way back to town. There were things Amy wanted to say to him, but the words just wouldn't come. He liked her, but what did that mean? How did she feel about him?

Maybe she was buying into Hannah's fantasy, searching for a

Prince Charming who only existed in stories. In her daydreams, she always found the man for her on an exotic cruise or a tour of a faraway country. His words hurt because there was a tiny bit of truth in them. Maybe she was too comfortable in her hometown, surrounded by family and people she cared about, but she wasn't threatened by Dr. Prince.

She wasn't.

CHAPTER 12

"I saw Dr. Prince," Hannah said, racing up to Amy when she brought her laundry to her mother's house after work on Friday.

"That's nice," Amy said. "Were you sick?"

"No, I saw him at the library. I told him about Snow White and Prince Charming. He thought it was a really cool story."

"Where's your Mommy today?" She knew her mother loved having Hannah stay with her, but sometimes Natalie forgot their mom still worked full-time.

"She and Daddy went to Des Moines. I get to stay with Grandma until Sunday. Dr. Prince said I look like a princess. He said pretty women must run in our family."

"I'll bet he did," Amy said under her breath.

It had been nearly a week since the couples shower, and she still felt like breathing dragon fire when she thought of Dan. The more she mulled over what he'd said, the more convinced she was he was totally wrong. Far from living in a cocoon, she played an active part in the life of the town. She still enjoyed old friends like Josie and Gayle, not to mention her cousin Mandy. And she did date, maybe not often enough by Dan Prince's standards but she had several male friends. In fact, she was going out to dinner tomorrow night with Will Davis, junior partner in the town's only law firm.

Although he was divorced and a few years older, Will was a hot catch in the eyes of the town's single women. This would be their first date, although he'd asked her several times before. At first she'd refused because she'd just met Dan—big mistake considering how that turned out.

Maybe Will wasn't as handsome as the new doctor with his thinning blond hair and rather long face, but she anticipated a good time with him. He had a great sense of humor, and the buzz around town was that his wife had left him for another man, definitely giving him the sympathy vote.

Hannah held the door while Amy hauled her basket of laundry into her mother's utility room just off the kitchen. Her mother's house had enough rooms, cubicles, and closets to accommodate a family of ten. Both her daughters had urged her to sell it and move into something requiring less maintenance, but she steadfastly refused to sell the late Victorian house because it had been in her husband's family for generations.

"I thought I heard you come in," her mother said. "You don't need to do your laundry. I can run it through the washer and dryer for you. You probably have something better to do this evening."

"You work too hard already," Amy said. "I'll do it."

"We're going to play Pollyanna," Hannah said. It was an old board game Amy's grandmother had once played with her. Now Hannah loved it. "Will you play with us?"

"Maybe a game or two while I do my laundry," Amy said, always happy to spend time with her niece.

"Dr. Prince said he'd play it some time," Hannah said. "Maybe he'll come over tonight, and we can all play."

"I don't think that's going to happen," Amy said, trying to let the little girl down easily. "Doctors are pretty busy."

"Not in the summer," Hannah said in a solemn voice. "People don't get sick much when it's hot. Are you going to live in a castle when you get married?"

"Honey, I'm afraid there aren't any castles in Iowa, only cornfields." Amy busied herself sorting the laundry.

"I told Dr. Prince I'm going to be the flower girl when he marries you. He thought a yellow dress would be nice. What do you think?" Hannah pursed her lips thoughtfully.

Stooping to talk face to face with her earnest niece, Amy struggled for a kind way to let the little girl down.

"It's a beautiful idea," she began, struggling for the right words. "But sometimes people aren't meant to marry each other."

"You're beautiful, so you have to marry Prince Charming."

"Honey, Dr. Prince is a nice man, but I'm not going to marry him."

"Never?" Hannah looked so dubious Amy wanted to laugh. Instead, she gave her niece a big hug.

"Maybe I can be a bridesmaid at your wedding someday," Amy said with a little giggle.

Hannah frowned, obviously not liking that idea. "I think Dr. Prince is a little too old for me."

"You're right there." Amy stood, hoping her niece would be distracted by her favorite game.

By the time Saturday night came, Amy had lost enthusiasm for her date with Will. It wouldn't be fair to cancel, but she just couldn't muster any excitement at the prospect. After working all day, she was sure she'd be a poor companion.

Still, her date had made reservations at the best restaurant within fifty miles. The Corral was just outside a nearby town, and in spite of its Western theme, it offered fresh Maine lobsters, and thick Iowa pork chops along with choice cuts of Omaha beef. The meal was well worth the drive, but was she being fair to Will? He should be going out with someone who would appreciate his company more.

Maybe because she wasn't feeling up to the evening, she made a special effort to look her best. She'd only worn her little black dress with thin spaghetti straps once several years ago. It hugged her curves like a second skin, but apparently that was the latest fashion. The bodice was low cut and sprinkled with sparkly fake gems. Amy was her own harshest critic, but she had to admit she looked hot.

When Will came to pick her up, his jaw dropped.

"You look fabulous." He sounded a little breathless, but maybe he'd run up the stairs to her apartment.

"Thank you." She grabbed her little red clutch purse, calculated to add a little bling to her outfit.

Maybe she wobbled a little walking down to his snazzy sports car, but at least she felt more in the mood to go out, knowing she did look her best. It was possible she'd enjoy herself more than she anticipated.

*

When Belinda had shown up on his doorstep Saturday afternoon, Dan didn't know whether to hug her or throttle her. Now, after hours of conversation that led nowhere, he'd reluctantly suggested they go out for dinner.

The soonest he could get a reservation at The Corral, the only restaurant in the area likely to meet with her approval, was nine p.m.

"I'll have to shower and change," she said in the voice that used to send shivers down his spine. "Why don't you join me for old time's sake?"

"That's not going to happen." He turned away when she started to peel off the minuscule excuse for a dress.

"Don't you want to see what you've been missing?" she purred, reminding him of her bad-tempered Persian cat.

"I haven't missed you, if that's what you're implying. I'm going to the Windmill Motel to get a room for you. Then tomorrow you're leaving."

"I thought you'd be glad to see me." She tossed her dress on his couch, but he didn't turn to check out what she was wearing under it—if anything.

"I've talked myself hoarse trying to convince you it's over between us," he said, going to the door. "You were right when you refused to come here with me. You'd hate it."

"I didn't know I'd miss you so much."

Dan shook his head, using anger as a shield against her attempt to seduce him. She was as gorgeous as he remembered, but their separation had made him realize how superficial and self-centered she was.

When he got back, she was sitting on the end of his couch in her panties and bra, engrossed in working on her nails.

"Don't get polish on the couch. It belongs to my landlady," he said, going into his bedroom to get ready for the meal he felt obligated to buy for her.

The alternative was a cozy dinner for two in his apartment, and that was a very bad idea. He was usually slow to anger, but her melodramatic avowal of eternal love had been so phony, he was ready to kick her out. The only thing that stopped him was her father, a highly successful cardiologist in Chicago. His recommendation figured prominently on Dan's resume, and he didn't want to alienate him.

He took a long shower, mostly cold since Belinda had emptied the hot water tank that supplied his apartment. By the time he emerged from his room wearing his navy blazer—one she'd given him so he wouldn't look scruffy at some affair in Iowa City—she was wearing a red dress so short it made her legs look like stilts. The neckline plunged down to her navel, making the dress look like a bathing suit and reminding him of the gravel pit that served as a swimming hole in Heart City.

"Let's go," he said gruffly, not wanting to remember watching a sunset with Amy.

He hadn't seen her since the baby shower, even though he dropped into the drug store far more often than necessary. If she hid in the back room when she saw him, he couldn't blame her. He had been out of line making a kiss into a spectacle in front of her friends. At the time, he didn't know why, but maybe he was marking his territory in front of the local guys.

For whatever reason, he'd goofed. His thought was if he gave her some time, she might forgive him. He didn't have much hope that she missed him as much as he missed her.

"How far is this place?" Belinda asked. "I can't believe there's a decent restaurant within a hundred miles."

"Far enough," Dan muttered. Far enough so Amy wouldn't see him with Belinda. If there was any chance at all they could be friends, he didn't want her to get the wrong idea about his ex-girlfriend.

Dan insisted on taking his van, and Belinda didn't argue as she once might have. She probably didn't think there was anyone worth impressing in rural Iowa.

Surprisingly, The Corral was crowded, and they had to wait in the bar for a table to be vacated. Belinda kept up a steady stream of chitchat, apparently not noticing his indifference. He checked his watch every few minutes, eager for the evening to be over.

Years ago, he'd been kicked in the solar plexus in a game of flag football. He felt the same impact when he followed a hostess through the crowded dining room and saw Amy at a table for two with a guy he didn't know. Her date was leaning across the table, his hand on top of hers and his mouth going a mile a minute.

When the hostess laid two menus on a table, Dan moved quickly to seat Belinda with her back to Amy. He didn't care whether his ex-girlfriend saw her, but he wanted the chair facing her table.

"Fresh Maine lobster," Belinda said, scanning a menu while Dan's still lay unopened in front of him. "Probably freshly thawed. People here probably don't know where Maine is on the map."

Amy was laughing at something her date said when a server with a dessert cart blocked his view.

"I suppose I could make a meal of the Cobb salad," Belinda said, frowning at the four-page menu. "I can't imagine eating a pork chop thick enough to stuff."

"Order whatever you like," Dan said, his eyes still focused on a side-view of Amy.

"Well, what are you getting?" Belinda turned in her chair to see what was distracting him.

"Is the blonde someone you know?" Her tone was brittle.

"The pharmacist at the town's drug store."

"Oh, yuck, one of those little lab rats." Belinda crinkled her nose in a way he'd once found cute. He didn't now.

Belinda had majored in art history, something she'd never have to use to make a living, but it gave her something to talk about at cocktail parties.

Ignoring her snide remark, Dan watched as Amy stood and started walking in his general direction. She didn't see him at first, so his guess was she was headed toward the restrooms. She was only one table away when she looked directly at him and paused.

The date must be special. She was wearing a little black number that set his pulse racing. For a few moments, he forgot that Belinda even existed. Her blather went unnoticed as he met Amy's gaze.

"Hello, Dr. Prince," she said as she passed his table.

Dr. Prince! That was bad. He didn't want to introduce her to Belinda, but his heart skipped a beat when she went by with a faint trace of a smile.

When she wobbled a tiny bit on her spike heels, he wanted to race over and steady her. The dress did wonderful things for her backside, and he could hardly believe how gorgeous she looked. And all this was wasted on some guy with thinning hair and a girlish laugh he could hear from across the room.

"The server would like your order," Belinda said in a frigid voice.

"Oh, sorry." He hadn't even noticed the young man in a maroon jacket standing beside their table. "Make it the stuffed pork chop with baked potato and the vegetable of the day."

Whatever he ordered would taste like dust, so he picked the entrée most likely to irritate Belinda. Would Amy believe they were there to cement their breakup? Most women would storm off in tears in the circumstances. Could he convince Amy about how cold and calculating his ex could be?

What had he ever seen in her? She was thin enough to be a fashion model and prickly when she didn't get her way.

Slumping back in his chair, he knew he wasn't being fair to Belinda. After three years in med school, he'd been eager for a permanent relationship. He'd pursued Belinda because she was sophisticated and witty. As a doctor's daughter, she seemed to understand the demands of his chosen profession. It had hurt when she refused to come to Heart City with him, but now he realized how wrong they were for each other.

Especially since he was falling in love with Amy.

The thought shocked him. She was cute and lively, fun to be with, but he'd never put his feelings into words. What should he do about it?

"Have you forgotten I'm sitting here?" Belinda asked in a plaintive voice.

"Sorry." It was all he could say. He was on edge, waiting for Amy to return to her table—to her date. Was the guy serious competition? Would showing up here with Belinda be the nail in the coffin as far as a relationship with Amy went?

When she came back, she circled around the whole room to avoid passing the table where he sat. What did that tell him? Was she avoiding him because she cared or didn't care?

Apparently they were skipping dessert. As soon as she reached the table, her date stood and took her arm. A minute later, they were out of sight, but Amy wasn't going to be out of his mind anytime soon.

When their food came, he ate without tasting, contributing little to the listless conversation. Belinda was the slowest eater he'd ever seen, but eventually he was free to leave the restaurant.

He left her outside the door of her motel unit.

"This is the last time I'll see you, isn't it?" She sounded genuinely regretful.

"Yes, we were good together for a while, but I think we both knew it wasn't a forever thing." Saying it aloud make him realize how true it was.

"Have a good life," Belinda said, sighing and leaning toward him to plant a soft kiss on his cheek.

"You too. Drive carefully on the way home." He walked away because there wasn't anything else to say.

After he said good-bye to his former girlfriend, he was miserable for a reason that had nothing to do with their parting. Had he blown his chance with Amy? Was there any way they could work through all the obstacles between them?

He wasn't proud of himself when he drove by her apartment. The light in her window was out, but what did that mean? He didn't even know what car her date had driven, and it wasn't his style to spy on women, not even one he was falling in love with.

CHAPTER 13

"Would you mind making a couple of deliveries on your way home?" Bert asked Monday afternoon. "You can leave now so you don't have to work overtime."

"Glad to," Amy agreed. It had been a slow day at the store, and the air conditioning had been running full blast to make up for the sizzling weather outside. She was happy to get out of the artificial cold.

"Mrs. Greenwich needs her blood pressure medication," Bert said, handing her a white paper bag. "And the other delivery is here in town."

After hanging her white jacket in the employee area in back, Amy smoothed the pink tank top she was wearing under it and grabbed her big shoulder bag. Bert handed her the two sacks to be delivered, but she didn't look at the larger one until she was out in the over-heated interior of her car.

"Dan Prince!" she said, shocked to be charged with making a delivery to the doctor. She read the slips attached, surprised the prescription was for pain. There were other things in the bag, but she didn't want to tear off the staple to see what they were.

The big question was, why couldn't he come get his own prescription? Or send his nurse? She couldn't help being suspicious of his motive in asking for a delivery when he lived only blocks away.

A few minutes ago, she'd been in a happy mood, feeling like a kid let out of school early. Now she was sure Bert had deliberately failed to mention who got the second delivery. Had he tuned into the gossip about her and the doctor? Did he think he was playing cupid? And what excuse did Dan have for asking for home delivery of a prescription?

First, she had to deliver Mrs. Greenwich's pills. At around ninety-eight or ninety-nine, she was certainly in the running for oldest person in the county. Even more amazing, she lived alone on a small section of what had once been the family farm. Her one surviving son had removed the back part of the original house and made it into a small cottage.

Amy knew the way, ending up on a long road where she had to drive with extreme care to avoid potholes and loose gravel. She knew from past visits that Mrs. Greenwich's son lived in another town and was constantly urging his mother to live with him or move to a nursing home.

When she got there, Amy knocked several times on the frame of the screen door, finally calling out through the mesh.

"Coming, coming, coming," the elderly woman said, clutching her cane and shuffling toward the door in bedroom slippers.

"I have your prescription from Warner's Drug Store."

"Silly to be taking pills at my age," she said when Amy handed her the bag. "If my son didn't insist on hauling me halfway across the county to see that quack doctor of his, I'd forget about them. What do you think of the new boy?"

It took Amy a moment to realize she meant the new doctor.

"I'm sure he's very competent." She thought about Dan a lot, but not about his medical qualifications.

"Competent!" Mrs. Greenwich scoffed, still standing in the open doorway. On some deliveries, she invited Amy inside and talked a blue streak, but it didn't look like this would be one of those times. "There's a word I'd rather not hear. My son doesn't think I'm competent to live alone. I'd rather share a stall with our old bull Rusty than live with that wife of his. Never liked her and never will. What do I owe you?"

"It's all taken care of," Amy said, trying to be vague because her son was in charge of all her finances now that his mother's vision was failing. "Do you want me to count out the first week in your pill holder?"

"I can still count to seven," the elderly lady snapped. "Thank you for coming all the way out here." The screen door banged shut behind her as she disappeared into the dim interior of the small house.

Much as she'd like to offer help to their oldest customer, Amy knew from experience the woman's pride wouldn't let her accept any kind of assistance. She drove back down the pitted road, saddened by the brief visit. Mrs. Greenwich had outlived almost everyone she'd ever known: her parents, siblings if she'd ever had any, her husband, and all but one of her children. No doubt her friends had all passed on too.

When the realization hit her, Amy stopped the car in shock. That could be her at some future time. If she outlived her sister, her mother, even her friends, who would be left in her life? Her darling niece Hannah would grow old too, hopefully with a Prince Charming of her own, but would she stay in Heart City where jobs were scarce?

After being lost in thought for several moments, she eased the car forward, but her mind wasn't on the pitfalls in the road. Instead, she could see herself growing old alone, perhaps still a part of the community but without the close ties of a husband or children. It suddenly seemed like a very bleak future, one she saw no way of altering. Her plan to take mythical vacations and meet the man of her dreams was no more realistic than Hannah's belief in a Prince Charming.

*

Dan hobbled across the room to get a bottle of water from the fridge, but it was empty except for some sad leftovers and condiments with nothing to put them on. Bert Warner had promised him speedy delivery of his prescription and supplies, but he must have a different idea about what was fast.

Painfully favoring his sprained ankle, Dan got a glass and filled it with tap water, although he still wasn't used to the slightly metallic taste. Of all the dumb things he'd done in his life, climbing a tree ranked at the top.

Back on the couch, he elevated his foot on a pillow and replaced the improvised ice pack, only a bread bag filled with cubes from one of the trays in the small freezer compartment. No surprise, it was leaking. He sank back, thinking unkind thoughts about the pharmacist, his store, the town, and Iowa in general.

"Don't be a jerk," he told himself. His ankle hurt like hell, but he wasn't in unbearable pain. He was hoping Amy would deliver his supplies, and the suspense about whether she would was worse than his physical discomfort.

When she finally knocked on his door, he was quick to call out. "Come in. The door's not locked."

He leaned back, rested his head on the arm of the couch, and hoped he looked pathetic enough to gain her sympathy, childish as he knew that to be.

"What on earth happened to you?" she asked when she stepped inside and saw him.

"Just a little fall." He tried to sound manly and unconcerned, but did he detect a whine in his voice?

"Your ankle is the size of a basketball," she said, coming close to see.

"I would've said a football." He tried to sound funny.

"Well, whatever, it looks awful. Where did you fall?" She stood holding a fairly large white bag.

"Do you want the truth or the edited version?" He knew he was going to sound like an idiot either way.

"Just tell me what happened." She sounded stern, reminding him of a nurse with an uncooperative patient.

"I couldn't sleep." No way was he going to tell her why. He hadn't had a full night's rest since he saw her in the restaurant with the skinny blond guy.

"And?"

"I still had hours to kill before my office hours, so I decided to work on the tangle of vegetation in back of the house. I've heard kids playing on the other side, and I didn't want them to get in there and pick up a case of poison oak like I did."

"Why didn't you get your landlord to clear it out?" she asked.

"The couple who own this place are getting on in age. I thought I'd be doing them a favor. They said I could put the debris on their cart, and they'd haul it to the dump." He was trying to sound noble instead of idiotic.

"So you were out there trying to get more poison oak." She didn't sound at all sympathetic.

"Actually, I wore a hoody, sweatpants, and gloves. I had the rash threat covered."

Amy stared at his ankle as though she'd like to dissect it for the answers he wasn't giving.

"I fell out of a tree." There, he'd said it.

"Cleaning out brush?" She sounded skeptical.

"No, I wanted to see how far the undergrowth went. The kids' voices had sounded pretty close, but maybe it was because things are so quiet around here. I just wanted to scope out the situation before I plunged into the middle of it."

"Let me get this straight. You climbed a tree to see how much work you'd have to do. How high up were you?"

Who knew she had such an analytical mind? He tried to be cool, but inside he was squirming.

"Ten, fifteen feet, just high enough to see over all the shrubs. When I started down a branch snapped. I fell maybe seven or eight feet, just a little more than my height. I landed hard on one foot, and that's the result." He pointed at the swelling, already discolored and ugly.

"Did you go to the emergency room at the hospital?"

"Be serious. I'm trying to build a reputation here, not be laughed at as a doctor who falls out of trees."

"I see your point. I guess you need these supplies." She handed over the bag.

"My ankle thanks you," he said. "I went to the office, but it hurt so much I had to cancel my afternoon appointments. Ah, good, elastic bandage and an ice pack that hopefully won't leak. Yup, it's all here."

"Of course it is. We may be small-town, but we know how to fill an order." Now she sounded miffed.

What had he expected? Maybe that she'd smother him with concern and beg him to let her help him? He remembered Belinda in a dress that looked more like a swimsuit and knew he had a lot to smooth over. The question was, did she have the slightest interest in being friends—or more?

"I didn't mean to imply otherwise. Do you see a lot of that guy?" No point being coy when he really wanted to know.

"What?"

"The blonde who was losing his hair."

"That's not a very kind description of the town's up and coming attorney."

She looked anything but happy, but he'd brought it up and wasn't backing down. "Your date Friday night. Are you a couple?"

"Do you mean am I sleeping with him, engaged to him, seeing him six times a week, or gaga over him?"

"Something like that." Now he really felt like an idiot.

"I thought of that as our first and last date, but maybe he's exactly the kind of man I should get to know better. Anyway, you certainly got acquainted quickly—unless your hot date was someone from your past."

"It was Belinda, and I think you guessed that." How could he explain her and not sound like a liar?

"It doesn't matter to me."

Little Amy wasn't a very good liar herself.

"She came here thinking maybe we could get back together. It's not going to happen,"

"So you wined and dined her at the best restaurant in the county." She was trying hard to sound indifferent, but he wasn't buying it.

"She's not the fast-food type. Afterward I dropped her at a motel and said good-bye."

"Do you want me to get you more water to take a pain pill?" She switched subjects so abruptly, he practically stammered an answer.

"Please. And would you mind filling the ice pack?" He held up the leaky bread bag, and she gingerly carried it to the sink.

"You only have one tray of cubes. The other one has hardly started to freeze." She efficiently filled the rubberized bag and brought it to him along with the glass of water."

Watching her intently, he almost forgot about the pain. She was wearing white cotton slacks and practical work shoes, but from the waist up she was adorable. Her shoulders were honey-gold, and the slightly damp tank top hugged her torso like a second skin. Tendrils of dark blond hair clung to her neck, and he could imagine tickling her throat with his breath. She moved with grace and self-confidence, and he wanted nothing more than to pull her down on his lap when she came close.

"Here." She'd wrapped a dishtowel around the ice pack, something he appreciated when she gingerly lowered it onto his swollen flesh. "Now take your pill, one every six hours, not to exceed four in twenty-four hours."

When she held out her palm to give him the big capsule, it was all he could do not to press his lips against her hand.

"Now you have one more problem," she said, stepping out of range.

He felt amazingly free of concern now that he knew the guy at the restaurant wasn't important to her.

"How are you going to get dinner?" She stood, hands on hip, challenging him to come up with something that didn't involve her.

"Order out."

"Fine, do you need me to look up a number?" She handed him the cell phone he'd left on the coffee table.

"No, I have the pizza place on speed dial. I can't eat a whole one. How about sharing? The least I can do after you delivered this stuff is buy you dinner." He tried not to sound too hopeful.

"It's a courtesy of the store, a way to stay competitive." She sounded matter-of-fact.

"I still appreciate it. You could've refused to bring it yourself."

"Josie has a husband to get home to. Bert's knees have been bothering him. Anyway, I had to take a prescription out to an elderly woman. Bert sort of tricked me into taking yours too."

This wasn't flattering, but Dan was too focused on pain relief and her really spectacular breasts to dwell on it. What he wanted more than anything was to stand and take her in his arms. Maybe it was a good thing he wasn't very mobile. She'd probably run away if he made any moves. He wasn't back in her good graces. That was obvious from her pouting lips and defensive stance.

"What do you want on your pizza?" he asked.

"Really, I'm not hungry. Get whatever you want. I'll stay until it comes so you won't have to get up to answer the door. Then I'm leaving." She sounded so determined he didn't even try to change her mind.

Had he done enough damage control so they could at least be friends? Unfortunately, Amy had lodged in his heart, and he was fearful that a casual relationship wasn't going to be enough.

She left him with the pizza box open on the coffee table and a tall container of iced tea sweating on a napkin. He watched her go, relieved that the balding guy wasn't important to her, but not at all sure what the future held for either of them.

CHAPTER 14

Tuesday was the longest day of her life, or at least it seemed like it. Amy wanted to check on Dan in the worst way, but she couldn't leave the store until closing time at six. Bert had taken the day off to go to the clinic in Des Moines where he was getting therapy for his damaged knees.

"You're quiet today," Josie said when no customers were in the store. "A person might think you have something important on your mind."

"A person might be wrong," Amy said, trying to make light of her friend's observation. "You have to admit time drags when we're not busy."

"I guess it's just too hot," Josie mused. "People probably hate to leave home for anything they can get along without. What do you have planned for this evening?"

"Nothing," Amy was quick to say. All day she'd debated with herself whether to check on Dan in his apartment, but she didn't even know if he'd gone to work. Maybe his ankle wasn't as bad as it had looked yesterday.

With only an hour to go before closing time, Amy was delighted when her sister and Hannah came into the store.

"Hi, guys," she said, hurrying to the front to greet them. "What are you doing out on such a sizzling day?"

"Hannah had a play date at her friend Cindy's house," Natalie said. "It's so hot we decided to come to Aunt Amy's store and have root beer in a frozen mug."

"It's not my store yet," Amy said, bending to give her niece a big hug.

"Guess what, Aunt Amy? Dr. Prince is sick. Cindy's mom was supposed to see him today, but he wasn't there." Hannah sounded so worried Amy looked to her sister for confirmation.

"His office called to cancel. Cindy was supposed to come to our house, but her mother said the kids might as well play there," Natalie confirmed.

"I don't think he's sick, Hannah." Much as Amy didn't want to stir up her sister's curiosity, she didn't want her niece to worry. "He sprained his ankle. I'm sure he'll be better soon."

"How do you know that," her sister predictably asked.

"I had to deliver pain pills and stuff yesterday. Come on, Hannah. Climb up on a stool, and I'll get your root beer."

"Just a small one," Natalie said. "It's too close to dinner to fill her up."

Frozen mugs had been a specialty at Warner's soda fountain for longer than even Bert could remember. He'd tried to take them off the menu because the heavy glass mugs broke easily when they were kept in the freezer, but his customers had protested loudly. Amy was surprised Natalie was letting her daughter have one. She was a fanatic about limiting sugar intake. Maybe the heat had mellowed her.

A woman came in and walked back to the prescription counter, so Amy left Josie to chat with her family. As soon as she finished with the customer, Hannah rushed back to her.

"How did Dr. Prince hurt himself?" her niece asked.

Smiling at her concern, Amy wondered who had the bigger crush on Dan, her niece or herself.

"He fell out of a tree."

Hannah gave her a look that said, "Are you kidding me?"

"Really," Amy said. "He wanted to cut down old bushes behind where he lives so children wouldn't get into poison plants. He climbed the tree to see how much work he had to do."

"There are poison plants?" Hannah looked worried.

"Some plants can give you a rash, like poison ivy. But don't worry. There aren't any in your yard. Your daddy wouldn't let them grow where you could touch them." She glanced at the soda fountain where Natalie and Josie seemed to be having an earnest conversation.

"Will he be all better for the wedding?" If Hannah hadn't been so sincere, Amy would've laughed.

"Honey, there isn't going to be a wedding, not with me and Dr. Prince. Maybe someday you can be my maid of honor if I marry someone else." Unfortunately, even Hannah knew she didn't have any prospects.

"No, I'm supposed to be the flower girl. I get to carry a basket and wear a yellow dress."

Amy stooped and hugged her adorable niece, telling herself it was only a phase she was going through. When school started, she'd forget all about matchmaking and go on to something else.

Natalie and Hannah left, but a big question stayed with Amy. Hannah would get over her obsession with Dan Prince, but would she?

Now she knew Dan was still homebound. The least she could do was check to make sure he had something for dinner. His fridge had been nearly empty yesterday.

After she'd closed the store, her nerve almost failed her. Would she be sending the wrong message if she showed up on Dan's doorstep? What did she hope to accomplish? She couldn't quite convince herself she was on an errand of mercy, so what would Dan think?

It was much too hot to sit in the car debating with herself. The best plan she came up with was to check in and see if he wanted her to go to the market for him. She'd do the same thing for a neighbor or friend who was laid up. If the California doctor read more into her offer, that was his problem.

Everything was quiet around the big Victorian house where he lived in his little apartment, but he was definitely home. His van was parked in plain sight.

"Hello." She knocked softly, part of her hoping he was asleep so she could sneak away. This wasn't the best idea she'd ever had.

Surprisingly, he came to the door, looking dumbfounded when he saw her standing there.

"You didn't bring me any food, did you?" He hobbled aside so she could enter.

"No, but I'll go to market if you want me to."

"Look at this." He stepped aside and pointed at his kitchen table.

Amy's jaw actually dropped when she saw the assortment of platters, bowls, crockpots, and assorted serving pieces crowded onto the small surface.

"The fridge is practically full too," he said, sounding as overwhelmed as she felt.

"It looks like a funeral buffet," she said without thinking.

"Is this what people do in Iowa when someone dies?" he asked.

"Pretty much. The state motto could be: Let no event pass without food. That includes graduations, anniversaries, whatever. But I've never seen anything like this for a sprained ankle."

"What am I going to do with all of it?"

"Well," she said, trying to think. "You can't give it to anyone in town without hurting feelings. Also, you'll have to return the dishes. Maybe some will fit in your freezer. I suppose you could actually eat some."

"Yeah, for the next six months. Why did people do this?" he asked.

"Because you're nice and they like you? No, I must have someone else in mind."

"Thanks a lot," he grumbled.

"There should be names on the dishes. Let me see what you have here." She walked over to the table and stared down at a collection of casseroles, a crockpot of pulled pork, enough salad for a convention of rabbits, and Mrs. O'Brien's famous carrot cake with cream cheese frosting.

"It's only a sprained ankle. I'll be back at work tomorrow," he said.

He scratched his chest, calling attention to his state of undress. Apparently he was trying to beat the heat by stripping down to a pair of red-and-white-striped bathing trunks and nothing else. She could hear the window air conditioner laboring away, but it wasn't up to the ninety-five degree heat outside.

"Well, there's no surprise here," she said, focusing on the table so she wouldn't have to look at his silky-haired chest. "Dorothy Gallagher makes a tuna casserole every time someone sneezes. But she's over sixty and not predatory. Here's the one you need to worry about." She pointed at a cut glass bowl filled to the brim with shrimp salad. "Sara Perkins Hayworth Francollo Jones just divorced her third husband. I think this was intended to introduce you to her dubious charms."

Dan groaned and hobbled over beside her. "Are you saying all this food comes with ulterior motives?"

"No, of course not. People here are kind. I bet Mrs. O'Brien gives away a hundred of her cakes every year. The word got around you'd been injured, so people responded in the way they can. It shows how much they welcome you."

"Then why are you here? I didn't feel very welcome after you left yesterday." He stared down at her with dark penetrating eyes, forcing her to look away.

"I'm very happy to have a doctor in town," she said stiffly, not adding she wished he were a short, tubby man with adolescent skin problems, someone who wouldn't be keeping her awake at night.

"Look at me." It was a command. He reached out and ran his fingers over the side of her throat sending shivers down her spine.

She met his eyes and saw something new and exciting in his gaze.

"Do you have any idea how much I think about you?" he asked.

"I guess not." What else could she say?

"We've gotten off to a bad start." He ran his fingers over the back of her neck while she tried not to squirm.

"Is that what you call it?"

"Are you afraid of me?"

He hobbled closer until her vision locked on the strong column of his neck. She wondered how it would feel if she ran her tongue over his throat, up the jut of his jaw to his waiting lips.

"No!" She certainly wasn't afraid of the man, but she was terrified of what might happen if she let herself fall in love with him. Some women weren't born for romance. She'd given up on having a great passion in her life before he came to town.

"I don't know what the future holds for us," he said in an earnest voice she scarcely recognized, "but I do think we'll both regret it for a long time if we don't give ourselves a chance."

"A chance to what?"

"Get better acquainted as friends." He smiled wistfully.

"As friends." She took a deep breath and moved back a step. Was it possible to be friends with a man who made her heart race and her whole body tingle?

"Good friends," he said.

"We can try." Her voice was a hoarse whisper.

"That's all I ask—for now." He reached out and took her hand, gently kissing the tops of her fingers. It was such a sweet gesture. She had to fight back tears.

"Don't you need to elevate your ankle?" It was a lame reaction to his tenderness, but she felt too emotional to give sway to her feelings at that moment.

"Great idea. I've had enough of balancing on one foot." He moaned as he made his way to the couch.

"Do you want dinner now? I could fix a plate for you." She needed to do something concrete until her heart rate slowed.

"Only if you'll join me. I never did like eating alone. It reminds me of summers when Mom was at work and I was on my own. I can make peanut butter sandwiches thirty-two different ways."

"You're kidding!"

"Not entirely, but I have a secret. I like tuna noodle casserole. I'm the only person I know who does."

"I like it too," Amy said, glad the conversation had turned to something as simple as food preferences. She needed time to take in what had just happened. This was a side of Dan she hadn't seen, and she very much liked it.

After warming two of the casseroles, she filled plates for both of them and brought them to the coffee table beside the couch, pulling up a chair for herself.

"The good ladies of Heart City know the way to a man's heart," Dan said as he tasted his way through a plate with a variety of dishes. "How should I thank them?"

"Phone calls, emails, letters—it's up to you. Maybe you could put thank-you notes in the dishes when you return them."

"I didn't think about how I'd get rid of all those bowls and pans. Is there any chance . . . "

"I'll help, but the notes will have to be in your handwriting."

"Doctors have notoriously bad writing," he said.

"It's the thought that counts." She didn't really believe that. As generous as the donors had been, they undoubtedly wanted to know more about the new doctor.

"I can't thank you enough for coming over," he said when they finished eating. "It was a long, boring day until you got here."

Amy had an instant thought about Mrs. Greenwich, alone in her little house day after day. She had to do something nice for her very soon.

"I have an idea," she said, still thinking about the details. "I made a delivery to a very elderly lady who lives alone in the country. You'll never eat all this food. Maybe I can repackage some in disposable containers and take it out to her. It must be dreary to fix meals for one."

"You're a thoughtful person," Dan said. "Come here."

Without hesitation she went to him and let him pull her onto his lap. His kiss was gentle, sweet, and wonderful. He kissed her eyelids and murmured in her ear, exploring her face with his lips.

"Now you should put the food in the fridge," he said unexpectedly.

Amy knew it wasn't food that concerned him. He'd given her an unspoken promise to go slow, to know each other as friends before they reached a point of no return. Reluctantly she wiggled off his lap, leaning down to kiss him hard on his lips before she walked away.

He seemed about to speak, but she hurried to the kitchen and spoke of practical matters before he could say something he might later regret. Her whole being was filled with feelings for him, but she had to hold back a tidal wave of love. Dan was injured, lonely, and unhappy in his temporary job. If he ever told her he loved her, she didn't want it to be for any of those reasons.

CHAPTER 15

According to Dan's patients, the biggest event of the summer was the county fair. It was late August, and it opened this weekend at the fairgrounds outside of town. Surprisingly, he was looking forward to seeing livestock exhibitions and the grandstand show. It might even be fun to try the rides and the rigged games on the midway. No doubt it was because he'd be there with Amy.

Driving back from a routine hospital visit, he thought about spending Saturday at the fair with her. In the weeks since he'd sprained his ankle, he'd seen her whenever possible, which wasn't often enough. His practice had mushroomed, keeping him busier than he could possibly have predicted. Now that people knew him, they were spreading his reputation throughout the county. He'd even had to hire a part-time receptionist to help his nurse Georgia.

He was late for their dinner date, or maybe date wasn't the right word. They hung out, took long walks, experimented with cooking dinner, and avoided the subject on both their minds: Where did they go from here? Dan wanted to be with her from the time he woke up in the morning until he fell asleep at night, but they both felt constrained from becoming lovers.

"We have to talk, Amy," he said as he drove, practicing the speech he probably wouldn't give.

The future loomed ahead like a big black hole. He was growing fond of his patients and the people of Heart City in general, but mostly everything he did was colored by his feelings for Amy. She loved the town and the people there. Could she be happy anywhere else?

As soon as he got to his apartment, he called her to say he'd be late. The weather had cooled down, and they were having a picnic at the city park with her niece. He adored Hannah and her fairy-tale imagination, and sometimes he even bought into it.

Amy checked her picnic supplies while she and Hannah waited for Dan. It had been his idea to take her with them, and she loved the way he included her family in their plans. Last week they'd driven to Des Moines with her mother for a concert, and he seemed to like her sister and brother-in-law too.

People saw them as a couple now, but were they really? There was something temporary and unsettling about their relationship, but she didn't want to talk about it with him. She was happier than she'd ever been in spite of the uncertainty, but she didn't know how they'd ever resolve their differences. Someday she'd take over the store. If she didn't, it might close forever and Heart City would be without one. She couldn't let that happen. What would people like Mrs. Greenwich do without the services Warner's Drug Store provided?

Anyway, she couldn't see herself working in a big chain store in California with customers she didn't know and corporate policy ruling her life.

"Aunt Amy, when will he get here?" Hannah was nibbling on carrot sticks, but she really did need her dinner soon.

"Dr. Dan has to take care of his patients. He'll get here as soon as he can," Amy said. "Why don't you tear this stale bread into little pieces to feed the ducks?"

"I don't like the big ones with green heads," she complained.

"You loved the babies when they were little. They're just the boy babies grown up. Anyway, we'll eat first, and then play on the slide and swing. Now remember what you promised. You're not going to say a word to Dr. Dan about having a wedding or being a flower girl."

"Okay," Hannah said half-heartedly.

Suddenly animated, Hannah was the first to rush to the door when Dan knocked. Amy was just as excited as her niece to see him, but she stood back and let the little girl be the greeter.

"Sorry I'm late," he said, handing a small bouquet of flowers to Hannah. "I didn't swipe them. My landlady said I could pick them any time for my two best girls."

Hannah had her mother's love for flowers and made a big production of putting them into a water glass. While she was distracted, Dan put his arms around Amy and gave her a long, slow kiss.

"I thought about that all the way back from the hospital," he said, his eyes saying even more than his lips.

"It's nice of you to invite Hannah to go with us," she said as the little girl carefully placed the flowers on her kitchen table.

"I get a big kick out of her," he said. "She gives me an excuse to act like a kid myself."

"You don't miss surfing in the ocean?" She regretted asking as soon as the words were out.

"Sure, like I miss volleyball on the beach, hot babes in bikinis, and skate boarding. But those are things I did when I was younger. Sometimes it seems a long time ago."

Amy didn't know whether that was bad or good, so she didn't say anything.

"What's for dinner?" Dan asked as Hannah raced for the door.

"Surprises," Amy said, hardly remembering all the things she'd thrown into the basket she'd borrowed from her mother. If it caught her eye as she went down the market aisles, she'd tossed it in the cart. She and Dan were learning to cook together, although she had to admit he had more flair for it.

"The peanut butter sandwiches are for me," Hannah told him.

"You mean you won't share with your favorite doctor?"

"You're the only doctor I know," Hannah told him seriously.

Dan put the basket in his van while Amy buckled Hannah into the booster seat she'd borrowed from Natalie. Her sister liked to give lots of instructions whenever she allowed her daughter out of her sight. It was a measure of how much she liked Dan that she'd only told them to have fun.

At the park, Dan helped her spread a plastic table covering on one of the rustic log tables in the park, weighing down the corners with things from the basket so they wouldn't have it flapping in the wind while they ate.

"Let's see what we have here," he said, peeking at the contents of a sandwich. "It looks like cheese and mustard."

"No, it's peanut butter," Hannah said giggling.

Everything tasted wonderful, even though it came straight from the deli section of the market. Dan convinced Hannah to try the potato salad even though she thought anything with mayonnaise was "yucky." Amy knew sharing a meal with him made everything taste better.

After they'd cleaned up and carried the basket to his van, Hannah could hardly wait to play on the equipment. Dan followed her up a ladder to the top of a slide that angled down through a big plastic tube. They both came down laughing.

"Give it a try," he called over to Amy.

"I'm not much on confined spaces," she said, but Dan wasn't taking any excuses.

All three of them climbed to the top, and Hannah went down first, giggling with pleasure.

"Our turn," Dan said.

"I really don't want to do this."

"Sit between my legs. I'll be with you all the way." He maneuvered her into position and let out a whoop as they slid down. Hannah was so amused she had to scamper to get out of the way.

All three of them were having so much fun, Amy forgot Hannah's bedtime. Most people had left the park as dusk approached, and Amy hurriedly called Natalie on her cell phone to say they were on their way.

"No problem," her sister said, surprising Amy. Apparently rules weren't important when Dr. Dan was involved.

After they dropped Hannah off along with her car seat and a partial bag of cookies, Dan drove to her apartment and stopped in a far corner of the parking area.

"I could make coffee," she suggested. Were they going to sit in the van and neck like a high school couple? That wasn't Dan's style.

"No thanks. I have a long day tomorrow. I have enough on my mind to keep me awake without caffeine." He reached over and caressed her cheek.

"Tonight was fun," Amy said. "Hannah adores you."

"She's a special kid."

He leaned toward her and moved his lips over hers, parting them with his tongue. His kiss was brief and left her wanting to be held in his arms. Instead, he backed away and looked at her with an expression she couldn't read.

"We've got to stop doing this," he said.

"Kissing?" She didn't want to understand what he meant.

"Denying how we feel about each other."

"Is that what we're doing?"

She knew it was, but she didn't know what else to say. Much as she loved him, she knew he would walk out of her life someday. Would it be better if they became lovers? She was afraid it would be worse. That old saying, "It was better to have loved and lost than never loved at all," was sheer nonsense. How could she watch him leave Heart City and still believe there was a Prince Charming for her?

"I'll walk you to your door," he said with resignation. "We'll talk another time."

After Dan left her at the door, her little apartment seemed empty and lonely. For better or worse, he'd changed her life forever. She didn't have a clue what she'd do without him after he left. Was there any future at all for them?

Sitting on the edge of her bed, too despondent to go through the motions of getting ready to sleep, Amy tried to sort out what was really important in her life. She focused on her family, her job, and her friends, but she was only kidding herself. She was in love with Dan, but she couldn't see a happily-ever-after future.

CHAPTER 16

Amy had never spent so much time in a cattle barn or enjoyed it so much.

"How long does it take you to care for Queen Bess every day?" Dan asked an earnest young future farmer whose entry in the competition was contentedly munching in a roped off area.

Wandering ahead because her interest in cows was fading, Amy mused over this new side of Dan. She doubted he had an avid interest in cattle, but he obviously connected with the young people who'd brought animals to the county fair. In fact, he loved kids of all ages, which only made her adore him more.

"How about some lunch?" he asked, catching up and capturing her hand. "Seeing the fair is hungry business."

"If you want a really good meal, the farm co-op ladies serve fried chicken to die for. Or we could hit the midway and try a corn dog or a burger."

"What do you like? Home cooking or lunch on a stick?" He put his arm around her shoulders as they left the barn, making their way through the Saturday crowd.

"I have a yen for a frozen banana," she said.

"You're kidding!"

"No, they're delicious dipped in chocolate and frozen. Don't tell me they don't have them in California." She bumped against him, trying to avoid a cone of cotton candy someone had dropped on the path.

He hugged her closer and bent his head to nuzzle her ear. Dan wasn't usually demonstrative in public, but the fair invited intimacy in an odd sort of way. Most fairgoers were so intent on experiencing everything the event had to offer, they were oblivious of what other people were doing. Of course, Dan was practically wearing a disguise: thread-bare jeans, a red t-shirt, sunglasses, and a baseball cap worn backward. She felt overdressed in a flowered skirt and a pink top with spaghetti straps, not that it mattered as long as she could spend time with Dan.

"I smell something wonderful," he said as they approached the food concessions.

"Onions frying on a griddle," she said. "The aroma is supposed to make burgers irresistible."

"You're irresistible," Dan said, dropping his hand to her waist. "Hey, let's ride the Ferris wheel before we eat."

They had to stand in line, but time flew when she was with him. Before she felt the least bit impatient, it was their turn to get into one of the open gondolas and gradually soar to the top of the wheel.

"Wonderful view," Dan said as they stopped at the top. He wasn't looking at the scenery.

"I love looking down at tiny people scurrying around," she said, feeling totally secure with his arm around her.

"I love looking at you." He leaned over and kissed her, and then did it again. "Wouldn't it be nice to be stranded up here for a few hours?"

"Wouldn't you get bored with the view?"

"Never." He pressed his leg against hers and squeezed her knee just as their car moved downward again.

After two more times around, their ride was over.

"That didn't last nearly long enough," he said.

"Good things never do." Amy wanted this day to go on forever, but she knew it wouldn't. The farmers would take their animals home, the carnival rides and concessions would move on to other fairs, and the crowds would forget about it until another year.

The fair had never seemed so magical, and Amy decided to enjoy it to the fullest, storing up wonderful memories for a time when Dan wouldn't be with her.

"Now what would you like for lunch?" Dan asked.

"You choose. I've been to lots of fairs, but you said this is your first."

"If that long line I see is for the fried chicken, I say go for the corn dogs," he said.

Amy didn't especially like the hot dogs on a stick baked with a corn meal batter, but today they tasted wonderful. So did the onion rings served in a paper cone and the fried ice cream. When they came to a stand selling funnel cakes, Amy begged off but Dan wanted to try them. He fed her bites as they walked until their lips were ringed with powdered sugar.

"Now what haven't we done?" he asked when they were so stuffed they were giggling about it.

"I'll pass on the wild rides," she said, not trusting her stomach after so much food.

"What about the Tunnel of Horrors? I don't think that will shake us up too much."

"It's usually a big nothing," she said, remembering the less than scary ride in past fairs.

"When I'm with you, everything is fun," he assured her, taking her hand and leading her to the ticket seller.

They were fortunate to get rear seats in the open car that would carry them through the attraction. A group of rowdy teenagers filled the places in front of them, but Amy scarcely noticed their loud comments and boisterous behavior. She settled against Dan, his arm sheltering her from whatever hokey scares lay ahead.

"If you get scared, I'll protect you," he teased.

The only thing that really scared her was the prospect of losing him, but she snuggled closer as the car moved forward with a rasping groan.

The boys in front of them were reacting to the spooky atmosphere with scornful hoots and loud laughter, but Amy was hardly aware of the headless ghost, the mechanical bat flapping down at them, or the zombie with fake blood. She and Dan were necking like kids on a first date, and she loved the furtive nature of their kisses and the shiver of pure pleasure that had nothing to do with phony horrors.

The ride was too short. Whenever she was with Dan, time went so fast it made her dizzy.

They walked out hand in hand, ready to wander aimlessly as long as they could do it together. Dan didn't seem to want to leave any more than she did, even though they'd pretty much exhausted the pleasures of the fair.

"What's that barn?" he asked as they passed a structure they hadn't visited yet.

"Looks like farm equipment," she said, not caring where they went as long as she was with Dan.

They stepped into the cool interior, but Dan's phone interrupted before they could wander down the row of shiny new machines, some bigger than tanks.

"Sorry, I have to answer," he said regretfully, stepping aside to let a family with small children in a double stroller pass them.

She knew. The phone had been a bulge in his side pocket all day, a reminder that doctors never really had a day off. It might be as minor as a patient with a skinned knee or something much more serious.

He checked call waiting and grinned broadly.

"Hello, Mom."

Wandering away to pretend interest in a huge combine, Amy gave him privacy to talk. Dan loved and admired the woman who'd raised him with only the help of his older brother. She felt the same way about her mother, so she understood how important it was for the two of them to keep in touch.

Their conversation lasted several minutes. When Dan caught up with her, he was grinning broadly and stuffing the phone back into his pocket.

"Good news," he said as she waited expectantly. "My mother is coming here for a visit."

"Great! When will she be here?"

"The first of September. She'll fly into Des Moines and rent a car. Leave it to my mother to insist I don't have to pick her up at the airport."

"How long can she stay?"

"She's taking a two-week vacation, but she wants to spend some time with my brother and his family too. I think she'll be here a week.

"That's so nice for you!" Amy was happy for him, but she was also eager to meet the woman who'd raised such a wonderful man.

"She was a little mysterious, though. She wants to discuss something with me, but she wouldn't give me a clue what. I guess I'll have to wait until she gets here. I have a surprise for her too."

"What?" Amy asked. Her biggest fear was Dan would find a way to end his work in Heart City before his two years were over. This was the happiest time of her life, and she didn't want it to end a single day sooner than the end of his contract.

"You," he said.

He took her hand, wandered over to a complicated piece of farm equipment, and pretended to be interested until a salesperson approached him.

"No thanks," he said to the company rep, linking his arm in hers as they continued their stroll.

She almost asked why his mother would want to meet her— why she even knew anything about her. But Dan's mind seemed far away, and she didn't want to say anything that might upset the tentative relationship they had now.

"Complicated business, farming," he said. "Some of this equipment must cost a fortune. A person has to have a lot of confidence in the future to make such a big commitment."

Amy walked beside him in silence. Was he talking about the chancy life of a farmer or their own future? Right now, she didn't want to hear anything that would spoil the joy of being with him.

CHAPTER 17

"You've been here four days, and I still don't know what your mystery is," Dan said as he ate delicious whole grain pancakes his mother had made for their breakfast.

"All in good time," she said. "We do need to have a long conversation, but we've both been so busy."

His mother was right about that. He'd been dealing with a late summer outbreak of chicken pox, and she'd been caught up in what he could only call a social whirl. The women in Heart City had not only made her welcome, they'd included her in enough activities to keep her busy day and night.

"Are you free tonight?" he asked with an ironic smile.

On her first day there, he'd introduced her to Amy and her mother, and from there it snowballed. She'd gone to a bunko group—he wasn't sure exactly what that was, but it involved throwing dice and winning silly prizes. His mother came home with a small figurine of a demented gnome. His nurse, Georgia, took her to a knitting club, and now his mother was clicking away on thick needles, making something that looked like an extra-long scarf.

The women in Heart City weren't just friendly. They'd adopted his mother and gone overboard making her welcome. He couldn't remember ever seeing her so bubbly and happy.

"Amy and Alice are taking me to an ice cream party this evening," his mother said. "It will give us a chance to get better acquainted, although I feel like we're old friends already. Of course, you're welcome to come too. It's a fundraiser for the Garden Club."

"I'll pass," Dan said, wondering if his waistline would survive a week of his mother's cooking. When he'd lived at home, she'd been too busy with work to fuss much over meals. Apparently she was trying to make up for all the salad suppers and take-out pizzas in one week.

"That's fine. I don't imagine we'll be out very late, although Alice did mention stopping off at a friend's house. She had minor surgery and is still recovering. There's a whole network of people looking after other people in this town. I've never seen anything like it."

When his mother smiled, the lines etched in her face seemed to fade away. The years of struggle raising two sons alone had taken their toll, but she was a beautiful person. Her hair was salt and pepper now, but it flattered her oval face and lively dark eyes. She was slender—almost too thin—but wore clothes with grace and confidence, even when she bought them at discount stores. Dan had always been proud of her. Now his heart swelled with affection. He wished they had more time to be together. Her visit was flying by, and he still hadn't had a serious conversation with her.

"I have to go to work," he said, getting up from the table. "When will I see you again?"

"I'll try to be home by nine," she said with a little grin. "But don't feel you have to wait up for me."

*

Amy was pooped. Her mother and Dan's had taken to each other like long-lost twins, and keeping up with them took all her energy. Fortunately, her mother took vacation time that week, so she was free to entertain Virginia Prince during the day.

That evening they were taking Hannah to the ice cream party. Amy didn't have time for dinner, but it was probably just as well. The Garden Club went all out for the make-your-own-sundae event. Participants could choose ice cream and syrup flavors and dozens of toppings. It would be a challenge to hold Hannah down to a modest sampling, and the homemade hot fudge was the stuff of dreams.

Her only regret was that Dan had faded into the background. She hadn't been alone with him for more than ten minutes all week, but, of course, he wanted high quality time with his mother.

Amy drove, stopping first at Dan's apartment to pick up his mother. She'd hoped for a few words with him or at least a glimpse of the man who peopled her daydreams and kept her awake at night, but she was disappointed.

"Dan had to go to the hospital," Virginia said. "Hopefully he'll be home when we get back. I'm afraid I'm throwing a wrench into your time together."

"Not at all," Amy said politely. "We're delighted you're here. My mom hasn't had so much fun in ages."

"She's a wonderful person. We have so much in common, both having raised children on our own. I can't believe we both wanted to be dancers when we were children, although I had to accept I have two left feet."

What hadn't the two mothers discussed? Amy was curious to know what they said about Dan and her. Did Virginia realize her son could hardly wait to get to California? She hadn't even told her own mother how poor the chances were for a long-time relationship.

The evening delivered on the promise of fun and good companionship, but Amy had to work to stay focused. She missed Dan even though she understood why he couldn't join them for an ice cream party.

"I want pink ice cream and chocolate sprinkles and cherries," Hannah said after they picked her up at home. "Are you going to have ice cream at your wedding, Aunt Amy?"

"Honey, I'm not having a wedding," Amy said, quickly interrupting her niece before she could talk about her plans to be a flower girl.

"Tell Mrs. Prince what you did last weekend," Amy's mother said, trying to stem the little girl's flow of words before she started talking about Prince Charming.

Amy was grateful, but she wondered what the two mothers discussed when they were alone. She knew her mother adored Dan, but did either of them realize how unlikely it was there'd be a happily-ever-after ending?

*

The longer his mother delayed telling him what was on her mind, the more curious Dan became. After he picked up take-out chicken and mashed potatoes, he went home to wait for her return. How odd was this, the son pacing while the mother partied? Worse, Amy was with her, so he didn't even have the solace of talking to her.

"I'm home!" his mother called out as she came into his apartment. "You can't believe how fancy the ice cream party was. I haven't had chocolate ice cream with marshmallow topping since I was a kid. I'll have to live on salads for a month to make up for it."

"Glad you had fun," Dan said, greeting her with a kiss on her cheek. "Tell me all about it."

"Later," his mother said. "I have something very important to discuss with you. I'll enjoy the rest of my visit even more when I've done it."

"You make it sound serious," Dan said, straddling a kitchen chair as his mother sat down opposite him.

"First a bit of sad news," she said. "Do you remember your great uncle William? He owned a grocery store in Stockton."

"Vaguely," Dan said, searching his memory to call up an image of a man he'd only seen once or twice when he was really young.

"He was my father's only brother. He died recently, but I didn't even know it in time to go to the memorial service his friends had for him."

"I'm sorry," Dan said. "Were you close at all?"

"Not really. He was a loner, in spite of success in business. I think there was some bad blood between my father and him, but

I never heard the details."

"Then you weren't affected too much by his death."

"Sadly, no, but he did something that will change my life."

"How?" It wasn't like his mother to tell him things in a roundabout way.

"Uncle William never married, and he outlived most of his close friends. When he made out his will, he left quite a bit to various charities, but he also mentioned me."

"You inherited some money from him?" Dan was pleased for his mother's sake but still didn't understand why she'd been so secretive about it.

"Quite a bit. In fact, I can help with your college debts now. You could pay them off and return to California." She studied his face for a reaction.

"No, that's not going to happen. I have things under control. Whatever you inherited is yours. I hope it means you can do things you've always wanted to, like travel and buy a nice retirement home."

"I'd really like to help you and your brother," she insisted.

"Tom will need money when his kids start college, but that's a long way off," he told her. "I'm a physician, Mom. I wouldn't dream of accepting money from you. You've done wonders for me my whole life."

"Well, maybe when you have children . . . "

Dan expected her to mention Amy since she'd already told him how much she liked her.

"I have some really big decisions to make," she said thoughtfully. "I'm thinking of retiring, at least from the museum. I want to do something different while I'm still relatively young."

"I think you should. You've slaved away your whole life."

"I'm glad you agree," she said in a solemn voice. "That brings me to my real dilemma. Where should I live?"

"I assumed you'd stay in California." The more she talked, the more puzzled he became.

"It's expensive to live in Santa Barbara. I've spent so much of my time there working and I really don't have a lot of close friends."

Dan could believe that. She'd spent most of her time when he and Tom lived at home doing things for and with her sons.

"You're leading up to something," he said.

"Next week I'm going to Tom's house to have this conversation with him. Then I have to make a decision about where to spend my retirement. I hope you can say something to help me make my decision."

"Mom, whatever you want to do is fine with me. I'd only urge you to take your time deciding. I'll be happy for you whatever you decide."

"I thought you'd say that," she said, smiling fondly.

After his mother went to bed in his bedroom, Dan was too restless to stretch out on the couch. He wandered outside, cell phone in hand, but he didn't call Amy as he'd intended. This was a family situation, and it wouldn't be fair to drag her into it.

His mother was so closely associated in his mind with the lifestyle in California that he didn't know what advice he could possibly give her. Maybe his brother would be more help than Dan was. Possibly his children would tip the scale in favor of living near his family.

Dan was weighed down by the necessity of making decisions. His medical degree didn't make him a sage, and he couldn't see the future. What he did acknowledge was the way he felt about Amy. He wasn't ready to settle down in California, but what did he want to do with the rest of his life?

CHAPTER 18

"I was sorry to see Virginia leave," Amy's mother said.

They were sitting on her back deck on a warm September evening, but Amy's mind was far away. She'd hardly seen Dan since his mother's departure early in the week. They didn't have plans for the weekend, and she was tired of thinking up excuses for his absence in her life.

Sure, he worked a lot. They weren't committed to each other in any formal way. He wasn't obligated to tell her everything he did. It still hurt when she didn't know where he was or what he was doing. She thought their relationship at least called for a courtesy phone message if they weren't going to see each other that weekend.

"She's a nice person," Amy said, knowing her mother expected some kind of response.

"I'm glad I could take the week off to show her a good time," her mother went on. "She said she hopes we can see more of each other."

"That seems unlikely." Amy didn't want to rain on her mother's parade, but the only way the two mothers would get together again was if their children married. Obviously, that was never going to happen.

"You never know." Her mother was getting as bad as Hannah when it came to matchmaking. At least she didn't call him Prince Charming.

"I think I'll go home now," Amy said. "I need to pay some bills, and tomorrow will be a long day at the store. Bert is taking off to visit a cousin in Spirit Lake. It will just be Josie and me."

"Well, have a nice weekend, dear. Do you and Dan have any plans?"

"No plans, Mom." Amy quickly left before her mother could ask more questions.

Back at her apartment, she slumped down in front of the TV

but didn't bother to check listings for a good program. She sat cross-legged on the couch, seeing but not taking in some movie with a fake-looking alien attacking a woman displaying her surgical implants in a military green tank top cut down to her navel. She wrote better dialogue on prescription bottles every day.

Enough was enough. She clicked off the television, but her thoughts were much more disturbing than a bad movie. It was so not like Dan to ignore her. Was he tired of her? Had he realized how impossible their relationship was? Was this his way of dumping her?

Crying would only give her a headache, and it wasn't as if she believed they had a future together. Clutching her cell phone, she checked for messages for the umpteenth time, but, of course, there were none.

When it was past midnight, she forced herself to get ready for bed. Even if Dan never called her again, she still had to go to work tomorrow. Bert was out of town, and a drug store had to have a registered pharmacist on duty whenever it was open for business. She was beginning to realize her dream job had a down side.

It was a shame Dan would never see the lace-trimmed ivory nightie she'd been saving for a special occasion. Nuts to him! Taking it out of the drawer and holding it up in front of the mirror, she decided to start wearing it. As soon as she slipped it over her head, enjoying the silky feel on her skin as much as she could enjoy anything, she heard the strident sound that meant she had a text message on her phone.

Would any man be crass enough to break up with a text? Probably, although it didn't seem like Dan's style. Dreading what she was going to see, she picked up her cell.

Hi, on my way to California. We can talk when I get back.

"That is the worst text message I've ever received," she sputtered angrily.

It told her absolutely nothing. Did he have a family emergency, or had he discovered a way to wiggle out of his two-year obligation to Heart City? Why couldn't he speed dial her number if he had something to say? The man didn't have a clue! Now she'd spend agonizing hours or even days waiting to hear from him.

"I'm not going to cry, I'm not going to cry, I'm not going to cry," she sang, trying to match the words to one of Hannah's favorite songs: "Old MacDonald Had a Farm."

She cried.

In the morning, her face looked like someone had used it as a punching bag. Her eyes had dark bags from sleeplessness, and her nose was red. Even using twice her usual makeup, she looked as perky as warmed-over oatmeal.

"Gotta hold down the fort," she said, using one of Bert's corny sayings.

In fact, Josie, a person not known for being early, was waiting outside the door when she got to the store.

"You must've had a big night," her friend said. "You haven't been late for anything since your dog followed you to school in the third grade. You were so upset! Taking him home spoiled your perfect record of never being tardy."

"Tardy! There's a word I haven't heard since—well, never. You, on the other hand, were born late. Remember when your dad had to drive you to an away game because you missed the team bus?"

"Hey, cheerleading wasn't my whole life," Josie protested.

"Could've fooled me." Amy unlocked the door and turned off the burglar alarm, trying to avoid looking directly at her friend. Sometimes a person could know you too well.

Business was slow on this lazy September day. Since the doctor wasn't available, she didn't have any new prescriptions to fill. By afternoon, no customers broke the monotony.

"Where is everyone today?" Amy mused as she and Josie stocked the painkiller aisle.

"Wow, where've you been all week? There's an Iowa football game. The whole town is glued to TV screens."

"Sure, I remember now that you mention it." She didn't have a clue what team they were playing. Only last season she'd been an avid fan, but so much had changed since then.

"That reminds me. Do you and Doctor Dan have plans for this evening?"

"No plans. He's out of town." Amy hoped her friend would leave it at that.

"Great! Brad is recording the game and having some guys over tonight to watch it. It's girls' night out for the wives. We're going bowling. You can join us."

"I don't think . . . "

"No, don't say it! When you lock the front door at six, you're not my boss anymore. I insist you come! How long has it been since you've had a wild night with the women?"

"You're right," Amy said, suddenly seeing no reason to sit home waiting for a call that might not come. "Girls' night out it is!"

"I'll pick you up around seven. We're going to risk the pulled pork sandwiches at the bowling alley for dinner."

Amy got home in time to change into jeans and a peasant blouse her sister had passed on to her, claiming it was too sexy for a mother. She scrubbed off her tired makeup and went whole hog in replacing it, determined to look cheerful. If she had it on thick enough for a clown, it didn't matter. Dan wasn't there to see it.

On impulse, she turned off her phone and left it on the kitchen counter. The last thing she needed was to mope around all evening hoping Dan would call. Whatever he was doing in California, he hadn't bothered to tell her. Let him wonder where she was!

CHAPTER 19

"We have a lot to talk about, but I don't want to do it on the phone. See you soon."

"Another darn text message!" Amy said when she checked her phone before going to work.

She wasn't going to answer. There was nothing she wanted to say in 160 characters or less. Dan had been gone a week, and he still hadn't called. His texts kept telling her how busy he was without a hint about what he was actually doing.

At the store, a few prescriptions had trickled in from a physician in a nearby town who was covering for him. But how long could Dan stay away from his practice unless he had some plan to cut short his time in Heart City?

"We're having another girls' night out this evening," Josie said Saturday morning. "Everyone agreed we don't do it enough. Can we count you in?"

"Bowling again?" She tried to sound interested.

"No, the Co-op Food Festival. It's gotten so big they've moved it to one of the buildings on the fairgrounds." Josie was energetically wiping the counter of the soda fountain between customers.

"I'm not much of a cook. The demonstrations aren't really my thing." Amy knew the worst thing she could do was sit home moping over Dan, but cooking?

"Forget them. We can watch the Food Network for that stuff. We're going for the samples. Mandy figured out we can feast for about the cost of a decent meal in a restaurant. I think it's only ten dollars to get in."

"What about husbands? Don't they like trying different things?"

"Have you forgotten the Big H?" Josie finished her clean up

and challenged Amy.

"It's not deer hunting season yet." She pursed her lips thoughtfully.

"No, but Brad and Mandy's husband Judson and some other guys are going to a hunting camp for the weekend. I guess it's legal now to hunt rabbits and squirrels, but mostly they like to pretend they're bachelors again. So, are you in?"

"Sure, why not. Maybe I can buy my mother a set of glass measuring cups for her birthday next month, especially one big enough to use as a mixing bowl. She saw one at a party she went to but thought it was too expensive."

"I imagine the party lady will have a booth there. Mandy's driving. We'll swing by for you around seven." Josie hurried to the front to help a customer studying lipstick colors.

When she got home from work, Amy wanted to go out about as much as she wanted a tattoo on her nose. What if Dan finally called to explain his absence?

"All the more reason not to be here," she said, deciding she wouldn't even take her phone with her after answering a quick call from her mother.

"Have a nice time at the Food Fest," she said, tactfully not mentioning Dan or his absence.

At first, Amy had been hurt by texts from Dan telling her nothing. Now she was devastated by the very real possibility it was over between them. She was crushed but angry too. No one could be as busy as he claimed to be.

She was waiting in the parking area when Mandy pulled up in her rusty old Buick with Josie beside her in the front seat.

"We're meeting the rest of the girls at the fairgrounds," her cousin said, launching into a monologue about her favorite topic: getting pregnant.

Tying to tune her out, Amy knew it wasn't necessary to carry on a conversation when Mandy was on a roll. Unfortunately, she couldn't stop thinking about Dan, even when her cousin gave a really funny description of the fertility chart she'd made.

The Food Festival was being held in the largest of the wooden frame buildings on the fairgrounds. The parking area in the vicinity showed how popular the event was, and Amy forced a smile, hoping it didn't look as fake as it felt.

"I hope Judson doesn't bring home some poor bunny rabbit and expect me to cook it," Mandy said, switching subjects without any prompting.

"Don't worry," Josie said. "If the men hit anything but trees, I'll be surprised. The hunting is just an excuse to hang out and be he-men—except during deer season. They take that seriously. We still have venison from last year in our freezer."

What little appetite Amy had plummeted at the thought of grown men hunting little creatures. Of course, she'd grown up without a father or brother, so the hunting culture was foreign to her. What did Dan think about it? Would he go native and try his luck when deer season rolled around? She knew so little about him! He was lodged in her heart like a barbed fishing hook, and she didn't even know his favorite color or how he looked without clothes.

They joined several others including the cheerleader who'd been captain of the squad their senior year. Now Zelda was a dental hygienist with the town's only dental practice. Her husband owned a service station, and she tended to lord it over her high school friends.

Amy found herself surrounded by a babble of conversation, none requiring more than an occasional nod of agreement from her. She loved her group of friends, even Zelda who'd once stolen a boyfriend from her. But she was the only single woman in the group, and the gap between her and her friends seemed to be widening. Would the time come when she'd regret returning to Heart City?

"Try this," Mandy urged when they stopped at a booth where a man in a big chef's hat and white apron was manning a small electric grill. Her cousin held out a chunk of sausage on a stick, and Amy lost it.

She couldn't stay there pretending everything was normal when she missed Dan so much. Shaking her head, she felt queasy and refused the morsel of meat.

"You don't look good," Mandy said, pushing up her glasses for closer scrutiny. "Are you sick?"

"No, just tired, I guess."

"Do you want me to drive you home? They'll stamp my hand so I can get back in." Mandy's concern touched her.

"Would you mind? I'm really not up to this."

"Of course not. Let me tell the others. They're over by the spice booth."

When Mandy hustled back, she led Amy to the door and outside.

"I really appreciate this," Amy said. "Sorry to put a damper on your evening."

"A few lost minutes means a few less calories," Mandy said in her usual cheerful way. "I didn't think you were feeling in a party mood when we picked you up."

Amy followed her cousin to the row where she'd parked, then stood stock still. Mandy followed her gaze and grinned.

"Guess I won't need to take you home," she said, falling back after nodding at Dan who was just getting out of his van.

"Thank you," Amy murmured as Mandy faded into the background.

Whatever she'd expected, it wasn't a huge bear hug. He swept her into his arms and kissed her so soundly she nearly lost her footing.

"That's how much I missed you," he said, backing her against the side of his van and capturing her between his outstretched arms.

"You didn't call me all week." She was breathless and a little dizzy from shock, but she needed more than a kiss.

"I couldn't." He looked shamefaced but didn't offer an explanation.

"Your phone was broken? No, it worked for texts telling me absolutely nothing. I forget—you aren't obligated to keep me informed of your whereabouts. What was I thinking? Oh yeah, I thought you'd left me for good, and I'd never see you again." She let all her fear and disappointment spill out in a confused jumble of words.

"It seemed too impersonal to tell you I loved you in a text."

"What?"

A group of teenagers streaked between parked vehicles without giving them a glance.

"Can we talk somewhere else?" he asked, opening the door for her.

"What did you say?" She wasn't sure what he wanted.

"Get in. Do you want me to propose to you in a parking lot?"

Summer was fading fast, but the stars she saw weren't the heavenly kind. She stepped into the van, hardly knowing what she was doing, and watched in stunned silence as Dan walked around to the driver's side and sat beside her.

"We have a lot to talk about," he said in a low voice. "Your place or mine?"

"Yours—no, mine. I don't know."

"Neutral territory then," he said. She suspected he was grinning but didn't look his way.

By the time she focused on where they were going, his destination was obvious. He didn't say anything until they were parked beside the gravel pit.

"Too cold for skinny dipping," he said, turning toward her. "I guess we beat the crowd."

He reached over and cupped her chin, gently brushing her lips with his.

"It's been a complicated week," he said.

"How complicated?"

"Let me start at the beginning. My mother received an inheritance substantial enough to allow her to retire early. My brother and I agree she should, after all the hard years raising us. That's where the negotiations started—and the reason why I had to go to California. Some things just can't be done on the phone."

"Like letting a person know why you left so suddenly," she murmured.

"Hear me out, please." He took her hand in his and caressed

the tender skin between her fingers. "My mother loved her visit here, so she decided this would be the perfect place to retire—warm, friendly people, low housing costs, lots of activities. And of course, her younger son is here."

"For now." Amy couldn't contain herself, but Dan didn't seem to hear.

"My brother hates to see her leave California. He has two kids and another on the way, and there's no question Mom adores her grandchildren. He offered to let her live with them. You can see how she was torn between living on her own and becoming part of his family."

"I hope you're going to tell me pretty soon what she decided." And what it means to you and me, she thought.

"She's moving here, but Iowa winters can be frigid. She'll spend two or three months every year with my brother, and the rest of the time here."

"But when you leave . . . "

"Hannah is a better listener than you are," he said, bending his head to kiss her.

As wonderful as his lips felt, she needed more. Curiosity was gnawing at her, and she was afraid to hope.

"I came to Heart City with a bad attitude," he admitted. "I imagined some hot career in Santa Barbara or another coastal city. Imagine how surprised I was when this town began to grow on me, especially the kids. I thought about how satisfying it would be to watch my little patients grow up. I want to see them playing sports, marching in the school band, getting married, and starting families of their own. You don't get that in a big city."

"You're going to stay here permanently?" She couldn't have been more surprised if an alien space ship had landed in the gravel pit.

"It depends." His voice was husky, and she could hardly hear his words.

It was the teeter-totter on the school grounds all over again. She remembered loving it when she rose up in the air, but it was always followed by a hard bump on her bottom when she plopped down.

"Depends on what?"

"On whether you'll marry me. I couldn't stand to be in the same town if we weren't together."

He reached across her into the glove compartment and pulled out a small box.

"Along with negotiating with my brother, helping Mom with a maze of paperwork, cleaning out her apartment, and kicking myself in the rear for not proposing to you before I left, I managed to pick out this."

He held the little box, turning on the overhead light so she could see it better.

"Amy Crane, I love you more than I can tell you with words. Will you be my wife?"

Putting her hands over her eyes, she could hardly believe what he was asking her. She'd gone from despair to utter and complete bliss so quickly her head was spinning.

"You're sure you won't regret your decision to practice here? We don't have to live in Heart City." She clutched her hands to mask their trembling.

"The only regret I'd ever have would be if you didn't want to marry me."

"No chance of that!" She tumbled across the gear box and landed on his lap, meeting his lips for a kiss sweeter than honey and ambrosia. "I love you, Dan Prince, even if you're not riding a white stallion."

"I'll take that as a yes," he said when she gave him a chance. "Your place or mine? We still have a lot to talk about—such as whether Hannah should wear a yellow or a pink dress when she's our flower girl. And how fast we can get married."

"October twentieth, my father's birthday. It's always a terribly sad day for my mother. This will make it a day of joy."

"That should give my mother time to move here. She wants to

buy a little bungalow—and we need a house big enough for me to chase you around."

Amy squirmed under a rain of kisses, trying to free her foot from the shifting handle. "My place. Put the metal to the pedal—the pedal to the metal. Oh just go."

"I love you, Amy," he said, helping her to untangle and sit in the passenger seat. "I won't be able to get time off for a honeymoon. Will that change your mind?"

"About you?" She giggled as he kissed her again—and again and again. "No way."

EPILOGUE

"I thought you said this was a simple wedding, just family and a few friends," Dan's brother, Tom, said, peeking out at the guests filling the church.

"It started that way," Dan said, nervously pacing in the confined space where he was waiting with his best man.

He fidgeted with the collar of his new white shirt, still starchy from the factory. At least he was wearing his own best suit and shoes that fit. Although he hadn't seen it, he knew Amy was wearing her mother's wedding gown. They'd started out wanting everything to be as simple as possible, but somewhere along the way, plans had snowballed. The whole town got into the act, helping in ways he couldn't have imagined.

Bert Warner was giving the bride away, and as a wedding gift, he rented the exhibit building on the county fairgrounds for their reception. With such a huge space, there was no limit on how many guests they could invite. Even though he and Amy had scrawled "no gifts please" on every invitation—designed and printed by her brother-in-law—gifts had been pouring in for weeks.

Her mother's bunko group had offered to provide fried chicken, and that was only the beginning. Their reception was going to be a huge potluck buffet, which was probably a good thing considering almost no one had declined their invitation. He had friends from seven states at his bachelor party, thrown for him at the vet's hall where he'd first met Amy.

His mother had gone wild planning the flowers as her gift, and Amy's friends from her high school cheerleading squad had decorated for the reception. About the only thing the town hadn't done was hold a parade.

"You're not going to pass out on me, are you, brother?" Tom asked. "I haven't seen you look so pale since you threw up at Disneyland."

"I was ten, and thank you for remembering," Dan said.

"I'm really sorry Kory couldn't come," his brother said. "Her doctor said she absolutely shouldn't fly in her condition. She's not going to believe this wedding. You've thrown it together in weeks when some couples spend a year getting ready for the big day."

"It just snowballed." Dan had a weird feeling, as though this wasn't really happening. What was he doing in the midst of this three-ring circus? Nothing in his life before had prepared him for this. He felt as if he were marrying a town, not just the woman he loved.

The church had a wedding planner on staff. Apparently, she doubled as the custodian, but she had the chops to plan a White House reception as far as he was concerned. When she gave him the signal, he and Tom stepped out to stand at the front of the church. His fate was sealed, and all the gray matter between his ears was numb.

The organist began playing the wedding march. He'd heard it often for friends, but the notes resonated through his whole body, awaking him from his zombie state.

Hannah started down the aisle, scattering yellow rose petals as she went. She looked like a little princess. Dan grinned at her as she passed, followed by her mother. Both he and Amy had agreed to stick with one attendant each, not wanting friends to have the expense of buying special clothes. Being a bridesmaid, Amy had assured him, was not much fun. She should know, considering she'd been wounded in action her last time out.

The assembled guests rose to their feet, and Dan's attention was riveted on the aisle. His trepidation dissolved as he watched the most beautiful woman in the universe glide down the aisle on the arm of her mentor. Head held high, she kept her eyes straight ahead, a sweet little smile lighting her face when their gazes met.

He loved her heart and soul. His life was beginning today.

*

Amy hadn't realized how beautiful her mother's wedding gown was until she tried it on herself. It was simplicity itself, high-necked with puffy short sleeves and beading on the bodice. There was no train, nothing to trip her up, and the veil was only a wisp of lace. Hannah said she as was as pretty as a fairy princess, and for the first time in her life, she felt touched by magic. Could this really be happening?

"I'm honored to play a part in your wedding," Bert said as they began the long trek down the aisle.

Amy tried not to look at her friends and neighbors as she moved between them. She wanted this to be one wedding where she didn't cry. Then she looked ahead and saw Dan watching. Her eyes grew moist, and she was afraid of losing it. How could something so wonderful be happening to her?

When he stepped forward to lead her to the altar, there was a fresh white handkerchief concealed in his palm. She took it and delicately blotted her eyes with her back turned to the packed pews.

The ceremony was a blur until they were truly married.

"I love you," Dan murmured when he took her in his arms and sealed their vows with a long, sweet kiss.

Hannah dropped her basket and ran up to hug them both. Dan took one of her hands, Amy took the other, and the three of them rushed down the aisle. A child had taught her: Sometimes wishes did come true.

*

Were brides supposed to nibble tiny bits of food at their own receptions? Amy couldn't remember the last time she'd eaten, and Dan did the honors, filling a plate to capacity for her.

"Think this is enough?" he teased, bringing it to the table where she was waiting.

"As a starter." When he was close, food receded in importance.

He sat down beside her instead of going back to fill a plate for himself.

"Aren't you going to get something for yourself?"

"In a while. All I want is to watch my beautiful wife."

"Eating fried chicken with my fingers?" She held out a succulent breaded leg for him to try and smiled when he bit into it.

"I adore you," he said, leaning close to kiss her. "Totally, completely. It's like discovering a new world."

"Umm, I never thought of you as an explorer." Laugh rippled out of her just because she was so happy.

"You will," he said, picking up a fork and feeding her a morsel of salad.

"The groom's only supposed to feed wedding cake to the bride." She cleaned the fork and slowly moved the tip of her tongue over her lips.

"Do that to me," he said in a sexy whisper.

"Oh, I certainly will, all in good time. First I have to throw my bouquet. It's tradition."

"Don't hit anyone. I refuse to do first aid at our wedding."

"Aunt Amy, when are you going to cut the cake?" Hannah rushed up with Dan's older nephew in tow.

"Soon," Amy promised.

"How soon?"

"Right now," Dan said, standing and pulling Amy to her feet.

Their cake was a castle made of sugar and love at the town's only bakery. Dan whistled when he realized they had to find a place to cut into it.

"There's a reason why I'm not a surgeon," he said, putting his hand on top of hers and letting her guide the knife.

People had gathered to watch and cheer, but Amy forgot about cake when Dan's lips slowly descended on hers.

"This is forever, my darling Amy," he whispered close to her ear.

"I don't think I could be any happier," she said when she had breath to speak. "I love you, my Prince Charming."

"If this is an enchanted land, I hope to stay here with you forever," he said, filling her ear with his words of love.

About the Author

Pam Andrews Hanson is the pseudonym for the mother-daughter writing team of Barbara Andrews and Pam Hanson. They have written nearly 40 books together and are still speaking to each other.

In the mood for more Crimson Romance? Check out *Love's Little Instruction Book* by Mary Gorman at *CrimsonRomance.com*.

www.ingramcontent.com/pod-product-compliance
Lightning Source LLC
Chambersburg PA
CBHW010641100726
47900CB00011B/2926

* 9 7 8 1 4 4 0 5 5 2 3 4 2 *